*To Francesca —*
*Happy trails!*

# WILD
# BLUE

### THE STORY OF A
## MUSTANG APPALOOSA

Annie Wedekind

Feiwel and Friends · New York

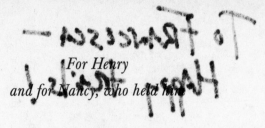

*For Henry
and for Nancy, who held* me

A FEIWEL AND FRIENDS BOOK
An Imprint of Macmillan

WILD BLUE. Copyright © 2009 by Annie Wedekind.
All rights reserved.

Printed in May 2009 in the United States of America
by Quebecor World, Fairfield, Pennsylvania.

For information, address
Feiwel and Friends,
175 Fifth Avenue, New York, N.Y. 10010.

Library of Congress Cataloging-in-Publication Data

Wedekind, Annie.
Wild Blue: the story of a mustang Appaloosa / by Annie Wedekind.
—1st ed.
p. cm.
Summary: After being captured by men, Blue the Appaloosa
grabs a chance at freedom and tries to find her way home.
1. Appaloosa horse–Juvenile fiction. [1. Appaloosa horse–Fiction.
2. Horses–Fiction.   3. Captive wild animals–Fiction.
4. Freedom–Fiction.]   I. Title.
ISBN: 978-0-312-38424-1
PZ10.3.W3765Wi 2009   [Fic]–dc22   2008034742

Design by Barbara Grzeslo
Feiwel and Friends logo designed by Filomena Tuosto

First Edition: 2009

10  9  8  7  6  5  4  3  2  1

www.feiwelandfriends.com

Dear Reader,

Welcome to the Breyer Horse Collection book series!

When I was a young girl, I was not able to have a horse of my own. So, while I dreamed of having my own horse one day, I read every book about horses that I could find, filled my room with Breyer model horses, and took riding lessons.

Today, I'm lucky enough to work at Breyer, a company that is known for making authentic and realistic portrait models of horse heroes, great champions, and of course, horses in literature. This beautiful new fiction series is near to my heart because it is about horses whose memorable stories will take their place alongside the horse books that I loved as a child.

This series celebrates popular horse breeds that everyone loves. In each book, you'll get to appreciate the unique characteristics of a different breed, understand their history, and experience their life through their eyes. I believe that you'll love these books as much as I do, and that the horse heroes you meet in them will be your friends for life.

Enjoy them all!

*Stephanie Mazo*

Stephanie Macejko
Breyer Animal Creations

# CHAPTER 1

THE RED HAWK CIRCLED, WINGS CATCHING a draft of warm air rising between the mountain ridges. Her keen eyes surveyed the land below, searching for a possible meal. A family of mule deer, thin and scruffy-coated from the harsh winter, tore eagerly at the early-spring grass growing in tufts along the hillside. To the east, dense forest swallowed the view, so the hawk swung into one more circle over the open land. She, too, soon would have a new family to feed. . . .

There! A telltale rustling among the leaves of the first spring beauties . . . could be a cottontail or a vole. . . . The hawk dipped silently downward for a closer look. She could see the small creature scurrying along its path, seeking its own spring meal. One more careful glance and the hawk would be ready to pounce.

Just as the hawk gathered herself for the kill, the quiet mountain morning was split by a piercing whistle, and a sudden thunder shook the ground. The rabbit (for it was a rabbit) leaped for his burrow, and the hawk retreated with a disappointed screech, flapping her broad wings to go in search of a quieter hunting ground. The cottontail, unaware of his close call, soon ventured back out aboveground—there was, after all, not much to fear from the familiar band of wild stallions now drinking deeply from the nearby pool of melted snow.

Like the deer, these four horses showed signs of a long winter. Their coats—dun, two shades of brown, and *grullo*—were shaggy and dull, pulled tightly over ribs without an ounce of flesh to spare. But their spirits were far from dull: Spring was here! From the snowmelt, icy cold and refreshing, to the new, tender shoots of grass and shiny buds of buttercups: Spring was here! No more would the bachelor band have to paw through snowdrifts in search of food. No more would they huddle deep in the forest among the rough trunks of tamarack and white pine, waiting out a blizzard. Spring was here, and it was time to play!

Thirst quenched, the dun reached out a foreleg and began to splash. It was still too cold for a full bath, but splashing was a fine thing. He was joined by his half brother, the dark brown stallion, and together they soon had half soaked themselves and their friends, raising a ruckus that drove the cottontail back to his burrow and put to flight a nearby party of grouse. The *grullo*–a blue-gray mustang the color of storm clouds with a long, sweeping tail and a dark stripe along his back, like the dun–pretended to be more annoyed than he actually was and charged at the dun: time for a chase!

In a froth of water and mud, the two young stallions charged out of the pool and up the rocky slope. Small in height but stocky and strong, they were evenly matched for speed, running heads high, their long tails like tangled flags behind. The dun wheeled to face the *grullo* and together the friends rose up on their hind legs and struck light, glancing blows with their front hooves. This play-fighting was preparation for later, more serious battles, when they would face older band stallions, herd leaders, in competition for mares. But for now, the young bachelors, having only recently left the herds in which they'd grown up, were happy to play together, forage together, roam together, and welcome spring with their bursting high spirits.

The dun nipped his friend's flank: Now I'll chase you! Back down the slope, nimbly maneuvering over rock and ice patch, the *grullo* bounded toward the snow-melt, where the two brown stallions were grazing, more interested at the moment in filling their bellies. They weren't allowed to stay on the sidelines for long—this time the *grullo* started the splashing, and the dun unceremoniously jostled his two half brothers into joining the merry mayhem.

An imperious whinny, blasting from the crest of the ridge, put an abrupt halt to the stallions' play. They had been too preoccupied to notice the presence of another, larger band of horses coming to water at the snowmelt. At its head was a strong-limbed, self-assured mare, shepherding her herd purposefully toward the inviting pool. And bringing up the rear, noisily announcing his family's approach, was the band stallion, no larger than the bachelors, but whose arched neck, flaring nostrils, and prancing hooves signaled his authority, his pride—his domination.

The four young stallions knew their place, and despite their interest in the fillies and mares who made up the rest of the herd, they beat a quick retreat away from the water, cantering far enough away to satisfy the band stallion, but still near enough to keep an eye on this interesting herd.

And an interesting herd it was. Each member, from the stallion now keeping a watchful eye on the distant bachelors to the little foal, born early only weeks before, wore a uniquely patterned coat of many colors, as individual as a snowflake. White spots, splotches, stripes, speckles, spatters—every lacy and dramatic design seemed to be represented, creating a dazzling display of nature's art. These were Palouse horses, named for the river their ancestors once called home. These were Appaloosa mustangs.

Even among this colorful band, two fillies stood out, at least to the young stallions sniffing the April breeze, hoping to catch their scent. They were half sisters, nearly identical in size, conformation, and bearing, and both boasted roan coats that would be nearly iridescent if not for their winter shag. One wore her mother's color, chestnut, shot through with white. The other sister had their father's coloring—black, which combined with the white hairs that make a coat "roan" gave her the color of rain, of water over rocks. In their own special form of communication, that was how this filly was known to her family—by her color. They called her Blue.

Blue and her sister, named Doe for her gentle disposition as well as for her bounding fleetness of foot, made their way to the water side by side, as they most often were. Behind them tagged their youngest brother, the new foal, a dark bay with a snowy blanket of white covering his tiny hindquarters and splashing down his hind legs. Rambunctious and bold, despite only having been in the world for a matter of weeks, he didn't let his unsteady balance stop him from skittering over the rocky hills, his long, ungainly legs flying, as he harassed each member of the band, from his indulgent sisters and aunts to his dignified father: Come play!

For the moment, the herd was too eager to reach the water to pay much attention to Fly, as the youngster was known. His mother turned and whinnied impatiently, urging him along. Finally the family was all gathered at the edge of the pool, their leader the last to arrive. He paused a final time to sniff the wind, survey the landscape, then lowered his proud head, with its distinctive Roman nose, and drank.

In between long drafts of the fresh, snow-tasting water, Blue cast sideways glances at the group of bachelors, standing a wary and respectful distance away. Like her mother, the herd's lead mare, she wanted to watch over and help guide the family, though she was far too young to take such responsibility. Her sister shared this instinct, though she showed it by helping to mother the foal and by giving contented, unselfish respect to the other, older mares—a sometimes cantankerous group. Through her gentleness, Doe commanded, just as Blue's alert eyes and fearlessness made her truly her father's daughter.

Blue was not the only Appaloosa with an interest in the nearby stallions. His thirst satisfied, Fly took advantage of the grown-ups' distraction and trotted confidently down the slope, his short, brushy tail flicking from side to side. Just as he reached the foursome, who watched his approach with curiosity, he paused and snorted, a tiny blast of challenge that fooled no one, then took another step forward onto a patch of slick ice and fell, legs sprawling out like a water bug's.

Blue could have laughed at her bold brother's ridiculous entrance, and the stallions looked on with expressions a human would have sworn looked like amusement mixed with sympathy. After all, they had been foals only a few years before. But Fly, only a little embarrassed, was already struggling to his feet, clumsy but determined. He began to prance a circle around the bachelors, occasionally darting closer to give one of them a daring poke with his muzzle, until finally the *grullo* gave in—and gave chase.

Keeping his strides short, much in the way an adult

human will let a small child win a race, the *grullo* cantered behind Fly, and then with a mighty bound he surged forward, cut Fly off, and changed direction, leaving the foal to pursue *him*. Up and down the rock-strewn slope they galloped, first one ahead, then the other—catch me if you can! Blue and Doe watched calmly, knowing that Fly was getting good practice, both in learning the terrain and in learning the language of stallions, of challenge and retreat, threat and response. It may be play now, but it would be serious later.

The dun and the brown brothers joined the play, and the pace picked up. Fly began to tire, and with the addition of the older stallions, the action was becoming rougher. Hooves and bared teeth, whirling and charging! The lead mare decided it was too much. Trumpeting a loud, clear warning, she summoned her youngest back to the herd. Fly, still trying to keep up with the roughhousing brothers, pretended not to hear. The mare whinnied again. Fly was almost sent to the ground by a shove from the light brown stallion. *Get back here, Fly!* his mother's call rang out. And when her son still didn't listen, Ollokot, the band stallion, charged forward.

Here was stallion language at its clearest and loudest. Chin slightly tucked toward his flexed, heavily muscled neck, ears pinpointed forward, straining with attention, the characteristic mottled pink Appaloosa nostrils blown open, Ollokot came on. He was a rough-looking animal, his eyes rimmed white, giving his expression a ferocious cast, the ghosts of old injuries lacing his body along with the white hairs painted down his hindquarters and back legs in slashing streaks. At ten years old, he was in the prime of his life, and he had defended his family against cougars and raiding stallions. Compared to these, the antics of a herd of adolescents, barely more than colts, were only an annoyance. Still, a display of power, even a minor one, was called for.

It only took one look at the charging band stallion for the bachelor herd to scatter. The *grullo* was the last to go, and he trotted away reluctantly. He respected the older, dominant mustang, but one day he knew he would challenge him. He cast a last look at the filly Blue, then turned to join his comrades.

Only one horse was unmoved by the stallion's interruption: the foal. Fly watched his new friends retreat up the hillside and let out a plaintive whinny. Ollokot grumbled impatiently, ears sawing backward. Fly glanced at him, as if to say, *What do you want, and why did you break up our fun?* Ollokot's head whipped forward and he gave the young horse a nip: *Don't sass me, boy!* Finally, Fly turned and allowed himself to be shepherded back to his family, unwillingness written in every slow stride. The only youngster not afraid of the battle-scarred, fierce band stallion was his son.

# CHAPTER 2

A S THE DAYS LENGTHENED AND THE SUN'S rays grew warmer, Blue's herd relaxed into spring's rhythm. Grazing, watering, playing, and even quarreling: Everything felt easier when the last of the long winter's snows had melted. And soon two more mares stole away from the band for a few days, seeking privacy as they brought forth their foals in the night's protective darkness.

One of these mares, an older bay with a lacy white pattern blanketing her entire body, had just returned with her newborn filly, a tiny, bandy-legged creature trembling under her father's curious inspection. Blue paused from grazing to watch her new sister, and after her father had covered the filly with his warm breath, gently nudging his greeting and his approval, she eagerly trotted forward to offer her own welcome.

The foal's Appaloosa markings covered her whole body, like her mother's, and she looked almost entirely off-white, except for patches of brown peeking out on her head, chest, and forelegs. Her mane, thin and tufted, was a zebra-like mixture of black and white. But more than her unusual coloring, Blue noticed the filly's tired air, and she whickered encouragingly to her. It was hard to be born, Blue knew, but even in spring the wilderness was not kind to the weak or the slow. She remembered this lesson well from Doe's brush with death, soon after her mother had given her life.

Doe had been born out of season, in November, five months after Blue. The snows had come, and Ollokot nearly prevented Doe's mother from going off alone to birth, as all wild horses are instinctively driven to do. Blue remembered his nervous harassment of the mare— a lovely young chestnut mustang with a delicate head that Doe had inherited, as well as her dished face and widely spaced, liquid eyes. Ollokot had lured the mare away from her family at a young age, and Doe was her first foal. One November evening, as the sun disappeared behind the ridge of hills, the mare grew more and more anxious to get away from the herd, but Ollokot kept bringing her back, blocking her with his body, neck long and sinuous like a snake as he nipped at her flanks, demanding she stay near and safe. The snow was deep, and the night wind cold.

But even these conditions and her mate's anxious bullying couldn't stop the young mare from following nature's instructions, and at some point in the long late-autumn night she slipped away from the herd to give birth to Doe. When dawn came, and the mare's loss was discovered, Ollokot went on immediate watch, as did Blue's mother, the lead mare. Instead of taking the herd to root for food in a new part of the mountain, the lead mare and the band stallion stood sentry, pacing the line of forest where the herd sheltered from the worst of the bitter wind. Blue, not yet a weanling but strong-limbed and steady on her feet, kept close by her mother's side, scanning the trees, the hills, the empty silence for any sign of her new half sibling.

Day turned to night and back to day, and still the young mare did not return. Finally, the herd had to move to a different part of their territory in search of food, but the band stallion lingered behind, trumpeting his call over the hills, restlessly pacing the high ground, sniffing the cold wind, searching for his lost mare. Blue tried to stay back with her father, but he drove her away, toward the herd and safety. Then he, too, was forced to abandon his watch, for he could not abandon his herd. But he did not allow the band to stray too far from where they were when the young mare had last been with them, despite their need to forage new ground. And he continued to search the skyline. His small, roan daughter, with her miniature copy of his Roman nose, also copied his movements, keeping her own watch, tiny nostrils flared open to scent the breeze.

On the fourth night after the mare's disappearance, Blue was woken from a light doze by a faint, faraway sound. She raised her head and listened, unsure what, if anything, she'd heard. The rest of her family was dozing, even her father, exhausted from his days of sleepless sentry. There it was again—a brief, high-pitched sound, almost like a bird. Blue's curiosity was alight, and despite the fearsome dark around her, she left the warmth of the herd's protective circle to investigate.

Moonlight shone through the needles of the white pine trees, making the crust of snow glitter and lighting Blue's path as she searched out the source of the sound. *Neee!* It came again, a short whistling call, and Blue picked her way forward through the trees. The voice, for she was sure now it was a voice and not the wind, was both familiar and strange, and Blue was afraid to call back, wanting to find but not to be found herself. She had seen a cougar once and had not forgotten its lantern eyes or the look of its white, sharp teeth, bared at her father as he drove the big cat away. And there were other dangers in these woods. . . .

The wind picked up, stealing through the fir and pine branches, and Blue raised her head to sniff deeply. There was indeed the scent of horse, and not a horse of her own herd, borne on the wintry breeze! Now she moved forward with determination, her mother's and father's instincts coursing through her veins, ready to meet whoever was lost on this winter night.

*Neee!* A small, unsteady figure stood in the clearing straight ahead, moonlight picking out the white in her beautiful coat of red roan. Unaware of Blue's approach, the foal let out another bleat, then hung her head down, struggling to stay up on her quivering legs.

*Neigh!* Blue's answering blast was hardly more mature than the foal's, but the exhausted creature lifted her head eagerly and immediately struggled forward, joyfully bleating with every tremulous step. Blue bounded ahead to meet the foal, and soon the two youngsters were flung upon each other's necks like schoolgirls, sniffing and nuzzling and greeting each other as the lost half sisters they were.

The look of surprise and wonderment on their father's

face when the two young foals emerged proudly from the woods to rejoin the herd was something that both sisters relished for their entire lives. The lead mare adopted the motherless filly, and ever since that night, the two roans, so similar yet so different, were never more than a few strides apart. The legend of Blue's boldness and Doe's endurance gave them a certain status among the other mares, young as they were.

But Doe's mother was never seen again. Her daughter never forgot her, and neither did Ollokot.

. . . .

**THIS WAS A HARSH BUT BEAUTIFUL WORLD FOR** wild horses, a territory unlike any other mustang habitat. Hidden in a northern Idaho wilderness, amid forests of Douglas fir and western white pine, cedar and hemlock, a handful of herds had somehow managed to find a small range so forbidding to travelers, so unlikely a place for a horse to live, that they had escaped capture and displacement for decades. They might not thrive here, but the hardy could survive. And the special pleasures of the snowy mountains—the tender grasses of the hidden valleys, the fresh snowmelt, the intoxicating wind—were such that few mustangs had ever enjoyed. They might not have hundreds of miles to roam, or rich, rippling grass plains to graze, but the Appaloosas and the other mustang herds of this unusual refuge had something more important: freedom.

To be sure, their presence had not gone entirely unnoticed over the years. Old logging trails scarred a portion of the surrounding forest, and the horses were accustomed to the occasional human. But whether on foot, horseback, or truck, the two-legged strangers usually kept their distance, and the band stallions, especially the fierce Ollokot, never allowed them close enough for more than a glimpse of their carefully guarded families.

It had been some time since Blue and Doe had seen a human, and now their concern was somewhere else entirely. It was an almost balmy day, the sun strong and warming. The sisters stayed close to the new filly and her mother, licking the foal's silky, pale coat, breathing encouragement through their delicate, mottled nostrils. The old bay mare was clearly anxious, and Doe gave herself over to grooming her mane and the top of her withers gently with her teeth, a soothing ritual of comfort that the sisters often performed together. While Doe took care of the tired, worried mother, Blue tried to help the youngster move forward. She could stand, but she seemed unwilling to walk more than a few shaky steps.

Fly wasn't much help, either. In his eagerness to play with his new half sister, he had knocked her over several times, and the sheer effort of returning to her feet exhausted the filly. Finally, Blue snappishly drove Fly away, and let the foal rest. Blue's gaze followed Fly as he half galloped, half tumbled down the hillside, in search of his friends the bachelor stallions. Blue spotted them before her brother did. They stood almost shyly on a hillcrest, motionless except for the breeze capturing and tossing their long manes and tails. The *grullo* stood nearest, and he was staring straight at Blue. Suddenly, he trumpeted to her, his bold, strong voice echoing through the hills. An almost irresistible response thrilled through Blue and an answering call rose in her throat . . . until she saw Ollokot glaring at her a few paces away. Feigning indifference, Blue turned her back to both her suitor and her father and lowered her head to graze.

Blue knew she was too young to leave her family herd, and she suspected that the *grullo* was too young to challenge her father, but she was curious about the bold stallion, so like her in color except that instead of the white swirls that marked Blue's coat, especially toward her head, where she became less roan and more absolutely spotted, he sported a dark line down his blue-gray back and faint dark stripes, like black lightning, down his legs. Someday, perhaps, they would meet and touch muzzles, trade each other's scent, and she would take the full measure of this wild horse, the first outside her herd to interest her.

This partial communication did not go unobserved by her sister, who now interrupted her grooming of the old mare to swing closer to Blue. Doe lay her head across her sister's back, her richly speckled neck and dainty freckled face almost pink in the evening light, a delicate contrast with the stormy gray coat on which she rested her chin. *Don't go.* And as Blue lifted her head from grazing, she nuzzled her sister's side in reply. *No, not yet.*

. . .

**THEM'S TWO PRETTY ONES, THE ONES STANDIN'** *together.* The man in the battered cowboy hat rolled down the window of the truck to spit.

*Scrawny runts. Ain't a real horse among 'em. They's all mutts,* his companion grunted from the driver's seat. *Where'd you hear about 'em? Ain't supposed to be no wild horses up here.*

*Fella at the gas station. Real proud of 'em, he was. Like they had this big secret up here that nobody knew about. I still say those two young'uns are nice lookin'. Folks'll pay for colors like that.*

The driver looked skeptical, wrinkling his nose as he drew his binoculars away from his pale blue eyes. *You think they're BLM horses?*

*Naw, the Bureau don't even know about 'em. I told you, that's what the fella said.*

*Hard to believe in the twenty-first century there are cayuse runnin' wild and don't nobody know about it, 'cept some local animal nutsos.*

*I'm tellin' you, that's what the man said. I was askin' about huntin' in the Wilderness, and he tole me to watch out we didn't run into the mustangs. Said this herd wasn't protected by the Bureau of Land Management like most other wild horses are. So if the BLM ain't protectin' 'em, they won't miss a few neither.*

*So whaddya wanna do? Have a roundup? How're we gonna do that with just us and this old truck? We can't drive over those mountains.*

*I got an idea 'bout that, but it's gonna have to wait till we get back to town. I can't have much of a discussion on an empty stomach.*

The blue-eyed man grunted again and turned the key, startling the old Chevy to life. In the distance, Blue and Doe heard the sound and threw their heads up simultaneously, nostrils flared. But it soon faded away, and they returned to grazing, feeling that the danger was gone.

## CHAPTER 3

EACH WEEK BROUGHT NEW SCENTS, NEW life, new sensations to the mountain valley. Now the hillsides were abloom with frothy lilacs that perfumed the air with the smell of orange blossoms, and grouse feasted on the flowers of honeysuckle vines that ran riot under the trees. Blue's herd wandered the breadth of their territory, shared with deer and the occasional family of bears and visited regularly by the band of bachelors, who still bowed to Ollokot's authority and kept their distance.

The mares and fillies were worried about Shadow, the new foal. While Fly was already imitating his elders and attempting to graze—though he could barely reach past his long legs to fumble at the grass with his milk teeth—Shadow didn't seem to get much nourishment from nursing, and tired easily. She struggled gamely to keep up with the herd as it made the circuit from graz-ing ground to watering hole, and the lead mare kept the pace slow. Indeed, everyone treated the pale little filly tenderly, even her boisterous half brother, who often suspended his play to settle down next to Shadow for a nap, flank to flank, in the warm June sun. While they slept, Blue stood nearby, on watch.

She'd shed the last of her winter shag some time before, and the brilliant spring sunshine burnished her coat till it shone like rocks at the bottom of a clear mountain stream—at least in the places where it wasn't caked with the mud in which she and Doe played after rainstorms. Her thick, tangled mane and brushy forelock were almost as black as her father's, and now, in her second year, her head, with its Roman nose, large, intelligent eyes, and pink muzzle, could have been a smaller copy of Ollokot's. Blue was not "pretty"—not in the way Doe was—but she had an unusual beauty of her own: a beauty shared by the wild outreaches of her landscape, by rock and rain and wind, summer lightning storm and black thunderhead.

Tenderhearted Doe was especially concerned about Shadow, and she was the most help to Shadow's mother in encouraging the foal to try to build her strength, and to keep up with the herd. Doe and Blue's help allowed their father and the lead mare to focus on guiding and protecting the entire herd of ten, from moving to new grazing ground to spotting cougars lurking in the rocky hills. It thrilled Blue to watch her father drive off a big cat, for, once spied, the cougar had no chance against Ollokot's slicing hooves and ferocious charge. Losing the element of surprise, the cougar slunk away. And so far Ollokot had never let a predator sneak up on his band unseen.

. . .

**SUMMER RAINS BROKE SUDDENLY OVER THE** grooved slopes of the hills, carved out from thousands of years of storms and snowfall. The highest peaks seemed to attract the black thunderheads, which released their weight in sudden, furious bursts that often ended just as quickly as they began, leaving the sky washed and brilliantly blue. But sometimes the rainstorm built gradually over the course of a dark, sullen day, heavy with clouds. On these days, lightning flickered over the hills like cold wildfire.

Neither Shadow nor Fly liked this kind of weather; indeed, a slow-building storm could set the entire herd on edge. On one such gloomy morning, Blue awoke from a light doze, the smell of electricity in her nostrils. A breeze was moving down the mountain toward the edge of the forest, where the herd had gathered in anticipation of wet weather, and it blew her mane back in ripples across her withers. She stamped a hoof, breathing deeply, nostrils flared, to see what was on the wind. She felt uneasy, with an almost foal-like nervousness about the coming storm. *Is it the storm*, she wondered, *or is there something else on the wind?*

Doe stood quietly by her sister's side, head lifted to the breeze. She watched as Shadow, lying almost between her mother's hooves, raised her head and began the slow process of untangling her spindly legs and climbing to her feet. Somewhat apart from the herd stood the lead mare and Ollokot, also gauging the weather and preparing for the morning trip to the water hole, some distance away. An eerie calm seemed to suspend the forest, the band of mustangs, the morning itself in a hushed state broken only by the raucous shrill of a pair of crows, who didn't mind rain in the slightest. Shadow, spooked by the nervous energy in the air and by the occasional crack of distant thunder, followed her mother with unusual energy toward the trail.

There was no sound—no *snap* or *crack* or *clang*—when Shadow collapsed. It seemed as though the little foal had simply tripped, as she often did, and her mother nudged her impatiently—*Get up now, we're going to water and don't want to be left behind*. Blue noticed that Shadow was pitched forward awkwardly on her knees, her muzzle touching the ground, one leg splayed behind at an unnatural angle, and she trotted over to investigate, followed by Doe. The sisters covered the filly with warm, encouraging breaths, and her mother nickered anxiously—the lead mare had struck out on the trail, and the herd was on the move.

Shadow struggled to pull her forelegs out from under herself. She was as eager to get going as the rest of the band. With her mother and Blue and Doe whickering over her, ready to help, she gave a great heave and pushed herself up and onto her feet, but a bleat of pain and confusion wrenched from her throat as she rose. Her right hind leg stuck out behind her with only the tip of the hoof touching the ground. Shadow looked backward at it, giving another high whinny. Her leg was trapped.

The snare bit a snakelike circle around her cannon, just above the hock. The wire was attached to one of the large, heavy rocks that were such a familiar part of the terrain. And though the mustangs couldn't see it, this rock was wedged between two even larger boulders. Shadow was going nowhere.

Confused, her mother nudged Shadow again, desperate to catch up to the safety of the herd. Shadow gave a gallant push forward and collapsed again onto her knees. Blue was perplexed: Obviously the young filly was hurt, but how? She saw the wire around her leg, and how it stretched back to the nearby rocks, but she couldn't make sense of it. Having only rarely seen any man-made object, the trio of mustangs had no way of understanding it or helping Shadow to fight it.

Shadow understood it. Shadow could feel it. It was a trap. It was binding her. And with the instinct of a thousand years coursing through her veins, tiny Shadow called up all her strength and all her courage and she rebelled. Again and again she threw her body away from the fixed point of the rock, straining forward on three legs until she fell with a cry of pain as the snare bit into her reed-like leg and blood sparkled up around the hateful wire.

The battle was awful to watch, and Shadow's mother trumpeted in panic to the rest of the herd: *Help! Help! Help!* There was wild fear in every note of her cry. Moments later, Ollokot came thundering back along the trail, mane and tail streaming behind him as the storm clouds broke and the rain came down upon his black-and-white back and the patterned backs of the small group of horses encircling the exhausted, shivering filly.

There was nothing Shadow's father could do. There was nothing any of the herd could do. For hours they stood under the driving rain, watching the foal fight and collapse, fight and collapse, fight and collapse, until her strength gave out and she moved no more, except for the labored breaths that trembled her sides and sent puffs of smoke from her muddied nostrils. She—and the rest of the herd—were caught on a fairly steep slope, and as the rain came down, the ground turned to a slippery sludge. Despite all the water, there was nothing to drink. And the lead mare and Ollokot knew that they had to take their family to water soon.

Blue watched her father pace a restless, frustrated circle around the band, forelock dripping rain into his white-rimmed eyes that flickered from his trapped daughter to the hills beyond, the lightning, the storm clouds. Blue shook her head, trying to no avail to rid herself of the damp. She felt stiff from her hours of fruitless vigil over Shadow. As the foal rested, she and Doe used their bodies to try to protect her from the worst of the rain and the mud shifting down the hillside. Shadow's mother was almost as exhausted as her daughter. She was an old mare, and the strain and lack of water were taking their toll.

Night fell. The band huddled closer together. And the rain came down.

. . .

**THERE SEEMED TO BE NO REAL DAWN IN THE** gray world that greeted the bedraggled herd that morning. The sky paled—that was all. The rain at least had paused as the storm clouds moved rapidly over the crest of the hills to the north. Blue broke from her position by her two half sisters to stretch her legs and to find her father. As she moved over the churned-up mud and slick grass, her wet coat looked patterned after the spring storm itself; it was as if she'd sprung from a marriage of the rocks and rain and wind. From the energy in her compact, leanly muscled body to the wild swoop and tangle of her dark mane and tail to the rough contours of her head and crested neck: She looked every inch a daughter of the wilderness. She didn't enjoy the rain, not like the crows who were bounding jauntily from their nighttime forest perches to feast on the grubs flushed out by the water. But storms suited her somehow, were part of her nature. She was cold and wet and sore—and felt just fine.

As she and her father touched noses, she could sense his worry: The herd would have to water soon, and if Shadow couldn't rise, she would be left behind. For several moments, father and daughter held a silent communion, then Blue abruptly swung away and trotted back to the still-sleeping Shadow and resumed her post. She lifted her head to Ollokot. *Go. I'll keep watch. When you return, I'll go to drink.*

The lead mare came to inspect Shadow. She gently nudged the filly, and Shadow raised her head. The lead mare nudged harder, and Shadow shifted upright. Bracing her forelegs, she tried to rise. After a brief struggle, she sank down with a groan. The lead mare raised her head and touched muzzles with her daughter and Doe before moving to the head of the herd, setting off on the trail to the water hole. Blue watched as, one by one, the dispirited, thirsty mustangs followed in her wake. Only Shadow's mother, Doe, and Blue stayed by the fallen foal, until Ollokot swung around and snaked his head at Shadow's mother, teeth bared, ears pinned flat to his head. She might be willing to die by her daughter, frail as she was, but Ollokot wasn't going to let her. His two-year-old daughters were strong. They could last some time more without a drink, especially with the wet grass to nibble on. Determined to move the rest of his family quickly, the band stallion barely cast a backward glance at the trio who remained behind. He would return for them.

An hour passed, and the rain started again. Doe and Blue grazed what they could from the mud-stained slopes, then returned to their posts over the foal, whose half-closed eyes and shallow breathing spoke her distress. The rain fell harder, and at a sudden crack of thunder, Doe spooked and half bolted toward the trees. Blue began to feel on edge as well. The storm's noise was jarring—the wind picked up and a confusion of wet and wind and thunder roll swept over the trio's lonely hillside. Amid the noise and the rain and the shifting winds, the sisters didn't catch the new scent coming from the old logging trail, farther in the trees. And they didn't hear the grumble of an old Chevy as it idled forward so its passengers could get a closer look at the rain-soaked band of sisters.

But when another crack of thunder shook the ground beneath them and Doe spooked again, bounding toward the water trail in an almost unbearable instinctual urge to join her herd, she could not miss the sudden, vicious bite of metal around her fetlock. Lunging forward, away from the pain, Doe felt as if her leg were stuck in a mud hole—something was dragging at her, slowing her down. She wheeled around and saw the wire connecting her to the stone, but didn't understand it; all she understood was that she couldn't move as usual, and she cried out to her sisters.

Blue was about to respond when, from the corner of her eye, she saw the man. He was standing behind a tree, staring directly at her. Blue bolted, hooves flying up mud and great handfuls of earth behind her as she swept toward Doe and toward the water trail and her family and the protection of her father until her flight was arrested by a small, plaintive sound that somehow cut through the storm's furious noise and the panic that filled her mind: Shadow's cry. Throwing up her head, Blue stopped. She looked back and realized that Doe was nowhere near. She'd managed to drag the great stone that tethered her leg partway up the trail but she could not run like her sister. And she, too, had abandoned her struggle to heed Shadow's cry.

Frozen, the sisters watched the man approach the foal. He called out, and another man emerged from the damp shadows of the trees. Blue snorted and pawed at the ground. The second man joined the first a few yards away from Shadow. In their hands they carried what looked to Blue to be long coils of vines. As they moved toward Shadow, the foal called again to her sisters—and Blue charged.

The men scattered at her furious approach, mud flying from her hooves, clouds of steam billowing from her nostrils. She could hear Doe behind her, fighting to keep up. Blue stopped between Shadow and the men, and the men stopped, too. They faced each other for several moments. Blue didn't know what to do, or even what sort of threat this was. She had only seen men in the distance; she didn't know what they did, how they struck. Her father had always run from them, driving the herd before him, and every nerve in Blue's body told her to run, run away as fast as she could. But what would happen to Shadow?

There was no time to think and barely time to react: The first man threw out his vine and Blue heard it whistle past her head. She bolted, springing like a cat to her left, then quickly putting her body once again in front of the foal. The rope sang out again and again and Blue leaped and pirouetted away from it while trying to stay close to Shadow. Several times she almost lost her footing in the mud and she came close to stepping on the frightened filly, but she didn't give up. Whatever this strange fight was, she would win it.

Then Doe went down. Blue didn't see it happen. She just turned and there was her sister, stretched out in the mud with a rope encircling her neck. She heard the cries of the men, though she couldn't understand them.

*I caught that purty one! I got her!*

*Tie 'er down and help me with this hellion, then.*

*Whaddya wanna do with the foal?*

*Might as well let her go. She looks half dead anyways. We can't mess with no sick pony. Now get yer butt over here!*

And then Blue felt the rope fall down, almost gently, over her withers.

She fought. Blue fought so hard that it took the weight of both men to bring her to her knees. She felt a prick, a sting in her neck, and gradually her wild thrashing slowed. She was so tired. Too tired to struggle as they forced her up the ramp into the truck. She could hear Doe's terrified whinnies, and then Doe was there beside her. Blue tried to raise her head to touch her sister's muzzle but it was such an effort. The strange world, the strange, dangerous world swam before her eyes. She could see the second man crouched over Shadow, worrying at the thing that had hurt Shadow's leg. The rain seemed to wash her vision out. And just as her eyes clouded over to sleep, Blue saw her father, running over the hill toward her. She lifted her head once, and then the world went black.

# CHAPTER 4

*T*HE GROUND SHOOK WITH THE ROLLING THUN-*der of the storm. Was it ever going to stop* storming? *She had to rise, to join the herd. How strange that she'd fallen asleep in such an uncomfortable position—slumped against this rock, her legs bunched awkwardly beneath her. And the smell... another animal had been here. Something with a harsh, unfamiliar odor. She had to leave this place, to find her father. He had been running toward her, hadn't he? Would he find her?*

As her eyes came into focus, Blue made out dirty walls hemming in closely around her. She wouldn't find her father here, not in this rocking, smelly, narrow place. She was half lying on a plank that had been thrust into the trailer, the rope around her neck twisted under her body. Blue wanted to rise, but the motion of the ground below frightened her. She felt as if the floor were threatening to split open, dragging her back into darkness. It had been so dark after the rope fell, after she stopped being able to fight. Blue had never had darkness come upon her like that before.

She listened for a while to the sounds that filled the unnatural cavity in which she'd woken. There was a regular *shush shush shush* and a confusing cacophony of creaks and rumbles. Sometimes the *shhhushhh* would grow louder, almost as if a wave of water were rushing past her cavern. And she could hear the wind—the one familiar voice. Light seeped in through a thin crevice in the wall above her. If she could get to her feet, perhaps she could see more clearly where she was.

Cautiously, Blue shifted her weight to the right, forcing her forelegs out from beneath her. The space in which she tried to maneuver was so small that her hooves scraped the wall in front of her. Her body didn't want to obey her: She felt weak, drained of energy, fearful. *Like Shadow trying to rise.* The memory of her brave, forlorn sister woke Blue up—*Where* was *Shadow? Where was Doe?*—and, summoning the unexpected strength of the small, pale filly, Blue braced her trembling legs and forced herself to her feet with a groan. And as soon as the sound left her, it was met by an eager whinny in reply!

Blue thrust her muzzle to the vent high in the wall to her right and breathed in Doe's warm, beloved scent, and she could feel her sister's breath just grazing her whiskers in return. Suddenly, her prison was bearable, for it was where her sister was. Her spirits braced with each breath she drew, Blue propped her hooves sturdily apart and stood straight, trying to avoid the slick spots of waste and water that pooled at her feet. Her legs shook with the effort to stay upright, but she did. Anything to draw Doe's comforting presence nearer.

But Blue did not forget to look across at the other opening in the wall that had first caught her eye. Whickering softly to Doe to tell her she was still close, Blue stuck her muzzle to the slats of the left-hand vent to sniff the outside air. It smelled of rain, but also of men—the smell of the Chevy, an acrid, bitter fume. Blue snorted with distaste and returned to her sister.

*Shadow?* she called.

*No,* Doe whinnied. *Only us.*

A great sorrow filled Blue's heart as she thought of her fallen sister and wondered what had happened to her. The men had apparently left her . . . but was she still trapped? Would their father be able to rescue her? Blue's mind swam wearily and she leaned against the partition between her and Doe, trying again to draw as near to her as possible.

She had no sense of how much time had passed since the rope had fallen around her neck and everything had gone so dark. Now that she was on her feet, reassured of Doe, and managing to stay upright despite her weakness and the treacherous rocking of the ground, Blue realized she was very, very thirsty. And this was the most perplexing thing of all: Never had she been physically unable to try to fill a need. She had never been not free. As this feeling swept through her, as strong and hot as her raging thirst, a terrible ache filled Blue's chest, a pain that had no physical source, and that left her so tired that she succumbed again to sleep.

. . .

## WHAT YOU BOYS GOT BACK THERE?

*Two of them cayuse you told us about. Trapped 'em up near the old loggin' road.*

*Can't have.*

*Why's that, old-timer?*

*Well, for the one thing, they ain't yours to take. For the t'other, those wild creatures wouldn't be caught, that's all.*

*Well, they was.*

*Lemme see 'em.*

A pause, then suddenly: daylight, flooding in behind Blue, making her turn her head so sharply that she rapped her muzzle on the partition dividing her from Doe. She swiveled her eyes and ears backward and could make out three shadowy figures lined against the glare that hurt her dark-accustomed eyes. Men. She could smell them, too. The smoky, sooty smell. With as much force as she could muster, Blue lashed out a hind leg once, twice, the echoing crash of her hoof against the metal trailer gate frightening her, frightening Doe, who let out a squeal as she, too, kicked back at the unreachable enemy just outside.

*Now you b'lieve me?*

*You had no business takin' those horses. They ain't yours nor nobody else's for the takin'.*

*Well, what good are they, runnin' around them mountains? They'd prob'ly just starve. They're all runty.*

*T'ain't runty. It's the way they're built—small and tough. Those horses been up in those hills since anyone round here can remember and they ain't starved yet. You better fetch 'em back where you took 'em from. I'd never have mentioned 'em if I'd thought you boys—*

*Just pump the gas, mister.*

*What'dja do, dope 'em? They got any water in there?*

*Mister, I'm tellin' you . . .*

*And I'm tellin' you fools that if you don't take those horses back, I'll call the law on you.*

*What law we breakin' by takin' varmint horses that don't b'long to nobody?*

*I'll think a one.*

*Outta my way, old man.*

To Blue and Doe, the words had about as much meaning as the growls and snaps of a coyote pack, but they could hear the anger building in the men's voices, and now they heard the sounds of a scuffle and loud curses, and they could smell fear and sweat. One man went down, and with a shout, his attacker slammed shut the trailer doors and all was dark again. Blue heard footsteps, the Chevy belched into life, and then the world's rocking began again, accompanied by the *shush shush* of the rainy asphalt outside.

. . .

WHEN LIGHT CAME AGAIN, BLUE'S THIRST HAD reached a fever pitch. A sour, rough coating papered her tongue, and she licked at the walls, hoping to find some stray drop of rain. She could hear Doe's labored breathing beside her and knew her sister was as thirsty as she was.

This time the lights that flooded through their cavern were not daylight but flashing, lightninglike blue and red bolts. Blue was torn between fear and thirst, anger and thirst, the need to run and thirst. She stood trembling, though the floor was still. A tall man, larger than any of the others, approached the trailer and shone another light inside, a light that danced around Blue's head like an enormous firefly.

*. . . follow you back to old man Ryder's place and call the Bureau from there. Don't think of tryin' anything.*

With the creak of hinges and a metallic clang, the doors shut and the dark and thirst returned.

· · ·

**THE THIRD TIME THE DOORS OPENED, THEY** stayed open. Night had fallen and the only light that reached the trailer was the yellow glare of the lamps illuminating the small parking lot of the gas station. Blue could hear crickets and the rumble of trucks from the distant highway. This time she didn't lash out when the doors opened. She waited to see what would happen next, and she kept her nose by Doe's.

*The man from the Bureau won't get here till tomorrow. You got a place to put these animals?*

*Pen out back should hold 'em fine. I put out water and feed.*

*If you say so, Ezra. You boys back this trailer up to the pen. God almighty, you're lucky we don't hang horse thieves no more.*

*Who we stole 'em from, I'd like to know?*

*Just back the durn trailer up.*

The doors stayed open, so Blue could partially see the strange things the trailer passed as it made its way slowly toward the small corral tucked behind the shotgun house that Ezra Penahwenonmi Ryder called home. The house abutted his gas station, off a highway service road, and it backed up against a scrub forest much like those that dotted the lower regions of Blue and Doe's range. Blue could smell the pine and the fresh night air and she whinnied plaintively to the half-familiar land.

Two men approached the trailer, and Blue pinned her ears back, recognizing the smell of the ones who had caught her. She breathed deeply, memorizing the enemy's odor. She would never forget. But as she inhaled, another scent pushed through the men's, the scent of something she'd been craving for so long that she almost feared it was an illusion: water! Suddenly, the lower half of the doors swung open, and Blue could feel the night breeze tickling her hocks. Behind her, surely, was freedom. But so were the men!

The rope around her neck tightened, startling her. The men were trying to pull her backward, and from Doe's shrill whinny, she, too, was being attacked. Blue threw her body forward, slamming her head against the wall in front of her. If the men wanted her out, she would stay in!

*That ain't the way to do it. I toldja to just let 'em smell the water and they'll come out on their own. I got a pot a coffee on in the station—let's leave 'em alone and see how they do.*

As the footsteps crunched away in the gravel, the men's smell lessened and the painfully sweet smell of the water grew stronger. Still, Blue waited, ears swiveling to catch the least noise from the darkness behind her, her sensitive nostrils distended. Pine and water and rock. The Chevy smell. Doe's smell. The lingering animal smell of the trailer . . . the smell of men. It was still there. But so was the water! Beside her, Doe was stirring restlessly, obviously as undecided and wary as her sister. Blue heard the thud of her hooves as Doe stamped and tried a tentative backward step. Still, Blue waited. She waited so long that she almost wore out the men's patience. But just before the coffeepot was drained and the sheriff and Mr. Ryder and the two grumpy cowboys eased out of their chairs, Blue's thirst won out over her caution. Slipping a little, she stepped back into the unknown—one, two, three hesitant steps— and then she lost her footing and slid the rest of the way down the ramp. Bounding up as her hooves hit dirt, Blue bolted away from the hated trailer, calling to her sister to join her, and seconds later, the mustangs had buried their muzzles in the cool, clear trough of water that the old man had filled in anticipation of his guests.

. . .

**MORNING BROKE WITH A CLEAR, PALE BLUE SKY** over the hills beyond the corral. The two young mustangs stood in the shadows of the white pine trees at the farthest end of the enclosure. Neither had touched the hay piled by the gate—after drinking their fill the night before, Blue and Doe had fled for the semi-shelter of the end of the corral closest to the forest, farthest from the men. There they had waited—for what, Blue didn't know. She didn't know any of the rules of this new world, so she stood on alert, tense and stiff from the hours in the trailer, trying to make sense of her new surroundings.

The men who had caught them had left in the night, and the smell of the Chevy and the animal-waste smell of the trailer were now gone. Blue could still smell men, and fire, and some sort of smoke from the buildings, and she waited, on guard in case they came back. She couldn't even relax to groom with Doe, who stood miserably pressed by the back fence, dried blood caking her fetlock, which was still encircled by the metal snare. The sisters drew comfort from each other's presence and warmth and smell, but their fear also kept them apart.

Both mustangs spooked when the screen door at the back of the house creaked open and Ezra Penahwenonmi Ryder, himself a bit creaky, eased down the cement-block steps to fetch the water hose.

*Mornin', ladies. See you ain't touched your feed.*

The sound was strange, of course, but the tone wasn't threatening, not like the men in the truck. And then more odd noises came from the lean, crooked figure, now ambling over to refill the water trough. Blue cocked her head and backed farther into the corner of the irregular corral, away from the man's voice. Mr. Ryder would have been the first to admit that his singing wasn't tuneful, but he hadn't intended to frighten the fillies. The sound continued, and the man came no farther than the trough, so Blue and Doe stayed put and did not bolt again. Eventually the man retreated back into his house, and the fillies began a cautious exploration of their new surroundings.

But the small, scrubby enclosure was not to be their home for much longer. After a while, another trailer pulled into the gas station's parking lot, and the voices of two new men came filtering over the warm morning air, along with the slamming of doors and rustling noises from unseen animals within. Blue caught the scent of horses and she froze, fixing her attention at the gate, though she and Doe remained in their shady corner. Soon three men approached the gate and leaned against it, looking right back at her. Blue bolted, racing down the far end of the corral, wheeling in the dust, and racing back to Doe. There was nowhere to run to.

*Where in the world did two wild Appaloosa mustangs come from around here? There ain't a Bureau of Land Management herd anywhere this far north in Idaho. That's a fact. There's the herd in Challis and the one in Owyhee, but they ain't got no Appaloosas.*

*I told you, two cowboys picked 'em up, and I think they was plannin' on sellin' 'em to the slaughterhouse. If they had a plan, which I sorta doubt.*

*But where'd they find the fillies, Mr. Ryder? That's my question.*

Silence. Blue shifted closer to Doe and nuzzled her sister's flank. The men continued to stare at them, but they hadn't moved yet, nor did they have ropes.

*I guess I don't know.*

*The sheriff said y'all had a band of Appaloosa mustangs up in those hills. A local legend, he said.*

*You'd have to ask Bud about that, then. I just want these*

*girls to have a good home . . . if they can't . . . get back to where they came from. You can make sure they get adopted?*

*Certainly try. They're interesting looking, that's for sure. Small, but those coats! Yep, they should go quick.*

*Wish I could keep 'em, but this place ain't set up for horses and I'm too old to mess with it.*

*Sure you don't want to tell us where they came from, Mr. Ryder? Bureau needs to know if there are wild horses on public or private land. There are laws about herd regulation and management, protectin' ranchers . . .*

*Sorry, mister. I just don't know.*

. . .

**THERE WAS, OF COURSE, NO WAY FOR DOE AND** Blue to know that Ezra Penahwenonmi Ryder was protecting their family's secret. Or that in order to do so, he'd had to sell their freedom.

CHAPTER 5

IN THE FOLLOWING DAYS, BLUE AND DOE traveled farther than they'd ever traveled before and saw stranger sights than had ever met their eyes before. Each hour of their journey brought new scents, new fears, new sensations, except for one crushing sameness about even the most unfamiliar experience: Everything was ruled by men.

They were now merely two fillies among a trailer of captured mustangs, and at first Blue's spirits rose when she was once more surrounded by her kind. But the other horses were as frightened as she and her sister. Doe clung to her side like a burr, resting her head on Blue's back as they helped each other keep their balance while the miles ticked by. The landscape underwent subtle changes, the hills softened, the smell of juniper and sage replaced that of honeysuckle. The air grew hotter, but at least in this prison they were watered regularly.

There seemed to be no use in trying to learn anything from the other horses. They shared the trailer with an older, swaybacked mare, obsessively focused on the sturdy foal who suckled vigorously even when the trailer banged and rattled its loudest. The mare was not from Blue and Doe's range, and she was the lone captive from her herd. She kept her distance, or as much of it as she could, considering their close quarters. When Doe attempted to give the foal a comforting lick, the mare turned on her, ears flattened with fury. Doe startled back, avoiding a nip, and did not make another offer of friendship. The other horses—a young stallion and two yearlings—were trailered ahead of the sisters, and all Blue could determine was that they, too, were strangers.

The trailer had stopped several times during the day's journey, so the mustangs didn't know when they pulled up to the stark corrals scattered across the flat, sage-scented plain that they had reached their final destination. The sun burned a fiery flare at the tops of the low-rolling hills that framed the horizon. Blue watched the evening light catch the dust that the jostling trailer kicked up as it made its way up the long, rock-strewn drive. This was a drier land than home, but still the sight of space, miles of it, and the smell of more horses livened Blue's spirits and she blew gently out into the air of early evening.

With a final metallic squeal and shudder, the trailer came to a halt and backed up to a shadeless corral a little larger than Ezra Ryder's. This time when the doors banged open, Blue didn't have to think: She sprang out in one shaky leap, bounding forward toward the empty space, the low-lying sun, the horizon that she had glimpsed from the back of the trailer. A fence stopped her. Blue whirled to the right: another fence. To the left: another fence! The space was just beyond, freedom was just beyond: Why were there now always barriers in her way?

Hours of exhaustion and frustration and fear boiled inside Blue as she whirled and whirled again, neighing wildly to the hills beyond, rising onto her hind legs to paw at the fence as men shouted and came running. She reared and plunged, reared and plunged, racing along the corral's border, crashing her hooves on the maddening barrier to freedom. She could think of nothing but flight—not even of Doe, until finally her sister's frantic neigh penetrated the hot rage that coursed through the mustang's body and brought her to a standstill. Doe neighed again, the sound filled with worry and lonesomeness. Breathing hard, sweat flecking her sides, Blue halted mid-flight. What, after all, was freedom without Doe?

. . .

**DAYS PASSED SLOWLY IN THE CORRAL. THE FIL-**lies, mares, and foals were separated from the stallions, who were penned across the road. There were ten male mustangs, ranging in age, some larger than any horse Blue had seen before and some even smaller and thinner than she was. It was the same with the female herd: There was an amazing variety of size, color, conformation, and temperament. Doe befriended several fillies and mares, including a long-legged, rangy bay who stood a hand taller than the Appaloosas, and a stocky pinto whose brown-and-white coat almost equaled the sisters' with its eye-catching design.

There wasn't much grass in the corrals and the horses had to get used to feeding on the hay provided in bales each day, along with fresh water. Blue wandered the pen, nibbling at the dusty spears of weeds, pawing at the dirt as if it were snow. So much of the mustangs' normal life was spent in the constant, comforting forage of food that it took her several days to make peace with the stack of hay that was easy to eat but tasted of the dry wind, not living green. And with each adjustment, Blue knew she became more of a captive.

By the end of her first week in the corral, she knew when the men would bring food, when the men would bring water, and knew the smell and sound and size of them. She thought that learning these things would help her and Doe. And yet with familiarity came a deadening of her senses—she was eating and drinking what the enemy provided her, and while she could not forget it, she still had to take what they gave her.

It was a shock when Blue first realized that some of the horses in the corrals allowed the men to touch them.

Doe's friend the pinto had picked up a stone in her hoof, wedged against the sensitive frog, and for a day she limped around the corral, trying not to put her full weight on the sore hoof. The next morning, the short, thickset man who always wore a hat, and who usually brought the morning hay, opened the gate to the corral and walked in, approaching the group of horses with a rope in his hand. Blue and Doe and several others spooked, darting to the farthest spot along the fence from the man. But a few mustangs stayed put, including the pinto. To Blue's astonishment, the man put the rope around the pinto's neck and led her toward the gate.

The pinto followed him calmly! Then the man ran his hand down the pinto's leg and raised her painful hoof off the ground, cradling it in his hands. Blue couldn't tell what he was doing to the pinto, but Doe's friend remained perfectly calm. Doe whinnied to her, and the pinto turned her head and whinnied briefly back. *Don't worry.*

The man put down the pinto's leg and stroked her neck. He removed the rope and the pinto trotted back to the group of mustangs huddled by the fence. Somehow, she was no longer limping. Doe sniffed at the odor of man on her friend, and jerked her head back, not liking it at all. The pinto seemed not to care: She strolled nonchalantly to the water trough, leaving the bewildered sisters to stare after her. But the new captives were soon to discover that they, too, were going to be handled by the men—whether they liked it or not.

. . .

IT WAS A HOT, DRY AFTERNOON, AND BLUE WAS dozing by the fence. She was dreaming of home: of green hillsides, the fresh smell of snowmelt, the sound of the wind through the tamarack. Sometimes the breeze that gentled the heat of the dusty corral carried with it a breath of the home-smell . . . water and rock, pine and rain. Blue sighed in her sleep. There was a scent the breeze could not carry: her family's.

Movement at the fence line stirred Blue awake. Instantly alert, she saw that a part of the fence that she'd thought was solid had been moved aside, creating a mouth that led to a narrow passageway. Blue couldn't tell where the passage led to, but she saw two men emerging from its entrance, ropes in hand. The men circled the mustangs, walking slowly and purposefully toward the rear of the group. Instinctively, Blue turned to face them, unwilling to have them behind her, where they were harder to see. The rest of the horses moved away from the men, walking the line of the corral.

One man moved to the right, the rope dragging along the ground from his outstretched hand. His pace was slow and deliberate, yet somehow he effectively blocked the mustangs' progress along the fence line, and now the pinto, at the head of the group, stopped uncertainly. The second man, stepping around Blue, approached from the rear, flicking his rope in the direction of the pinto's heels. With a snort of annoyance, the pinto trotted forward, through the mouth of the chute! Now the men moved faster, directing the rest of the horses toward the passage, and the herd broke apart. Three mares bolted directly after the pinto, the corral's default lead mare. Doe wheeled in place and cantered back to Blue, pinned at the opposite side of the corral. The old, swaybacked mare and her filly ran in circles away from the men, the mother changing direction several times to keep her body in between her foal and the men's ropes.

A sudden vision of Shadow, her brave, frail sister, lying helplessly alone as those first men bore down upon her, filled Blue's mind, and without thinking, she plunged forward to help the old mare protect her foal.

*Whack!* The sharp blow to her shoulder was so unexpected that at first Blue couldn't imagine where it had come from. But then she saw the rage in the mare's eyes as, in her panic, she turned on Blue and her sister, darting forward with her lips drawn back against her teeth, wild with the need to protect her foal from all comers.

The men took advantage of the mustangs' disarray. As Blue leaped aside to avoid the mare's charge, the brush of a rope across her pasterns drove her unseeingly forward . . . forward . . . straight through the mouth of the passage and into the narrow chute. She could hear her sister snort behind her and knew that she, too, was caught. Only the ferocious old mare and her foal were untouchable, at least that day.

What in the world was the men's purpose? Nothing that happened next made sense, and Blue fought: fought because she could not trust, fought because she was afraid. Waving their arms, the men drove her farther into the chute, and a door banged shut behind her, separating her from Doe. Another door swung closed ahead of her, blocking her escape. A rope fell over her head, hands grasped at her mane, her jaw. They did not hurt her, but they were men's hands, and she could not run. She struggled to break free, to break from their hold and to break from the narrow space that reminded her of the first place she was held captive: the hated trailer.

They were too strong for her. She had no room to move, no space to rear or to kick. Strong arms cradled her head, her neck. A soft voice, low and cadenced like Ezra Ryder's, spoke in her ear. Something was forced in her mouth, and the back of her tongue was coated with a pasty substance. Pricks of pain in her neck. Blue stood frozen, each muscle strained with tension. Then another sensation on her neck—ice, blazingly cold, startling in the afternoon heat. And then just as suddenly as it began, it was over: The door before her swung open and Blue bounded free. One of the men patted her quarters as she leaped away, down the chute, into a new paddock where the other mustangs were already chewing hay and swishing flies. It was almost as if nothing had happened.

But it had. Something had happened inside Blue. She waited anxiously for her sister, neighing toward the fence that separated them. Now Doe's fine head, with its whorls of strawberry and white and its delicate pink muzzle, was encircled by the men's arms. Blue could just see the white outline of her sister's eyes, wide with fear but latched on hers, drawing on Blue's image for strength. Finally, it was over—the last gate swung open, and Doe ran to Blue and the others, shaken but unharmed. She bore a strange mark on her neck, just below the crest where her red mane hung shaggily down. It was as if her Appaloosa coat had suddenly developed a new pattern. Blue remembered the sensation of ice on her own neck. She sniffed Doe, hating the smell of men on her, but needing the reassurance of closeness. And when she looked down, she was startled to see that the rusty wire that had clung to Doe's leg for so many days had disappeared.

As the sisters stood together under the glare of the afternoon sun, Blue thought that she hated nothing more than the smell of men. Men were fences and ropes. Men were the trailer and thirst. She suddenly knew, and knew it as strongly as she knew herself and her instincts, that she could not bear to have them catch her again.

This is what happened inside her: A rebel was born.

Before, with each new, bewildering event, she had reacted from fear, from her wild need to flee the unfamiliar and the threatening. But now she had learned things, lessons she could use with her instincts. Blue knew what humans wanted: to trap her and her family. And she knew that she must escape, whatever the cost. They would not touch her again.

# CHAPTER 6

ONE PARTICULARLY DRY AND SUN-SOAKED morning, a new sort of disturbance broke the monotony of life in the pens. Blue had just finished a long drink of water when she caught the fumy smell of trucks and heard in the distance the rumble of wheels jutting over the rocky drive toward the corrals. The recently captured mustangs—Doe and the old mare and her foal included—startled alert and moved toward the back fence, ears flickering nervously toward the commotion. The pinto and the other veterans cocked an ear and then settled back to swishing flies.

Soon the drive was a whirl of dust that cloaked a small troop of cars and pickups groaning to a halt under the blazing sun. Doors slammed, and the brown haze filled with the voices of men. Blue raised her muzzle and snorted. Not all of the men sounded the same. These were new voices, surely, and also different kinds: high-pitched tones among the low, and softer voices, too. Doe glanced at her questioningly, and Blue took a cautious step forward, sniffing the dust-choked air, determined to learn—a determination that more and more outpaced her fear.

*This here's the mares and fillies, and the stallions are penned across the road.*

That was the man who had roped the pinto.

A high-pitched voice: *Dad, can we go look at the stallions?*

A very low voice: *Sure, but let's take a look over here first. Your mom was thinking about a filly, and we should take some pictures of this bunch to show her.*

An even higher voice: *Look at the baby! There's a little baby one in there! Can I pet her?*

A softer voice, somehow gentler: *No, she's too scared just now. You have to make friends with them before you can pet them. Remember, these are wild animals, honey.*

*I thought they were ponies!*

*We-e-ell, they are, but they're wild ponies. Never been around people before.*

*Where have they been, then?*

*Free, I expect.*

By this time the dust had settled in the lot, and Blue could see the men approaching the corral. The familiar ones who brought the mustangs food and water came first, followed by several new men and . . . children. Men had foals. That was the only thing these small, high-pitched creatures could be. They gamboled and skipped much as Fly did, and their voices squeaked like Shadow's. Blue watched them come, fascinated. Smaller men with softer voices followed: females, Blue realized with a start. Men and females and their young. So much to learn!

As the crowd gathered along the fence, the grown-ups leaning their elbows atop the gate and the little ones scrambling for footholds on the rails, Blue took another step forward, drinking in the sweetish smell of the children. Their sudden, shrill squawks startled her a bit, but she stood her ground.

*Dad, look at that one! Look at those spots! We gotta take a picture of her for Mom.*

*Get a look at her sister, right there behind her. She's the best horse we got here, if you ask me. Found 'em together up north aways.*

*She looks like a show horse! That gorgeous strawberry color!*

Soft sighs of appreciation sounded along the fence line.

*That's the prettiest horse I've ever seen. She's like a rain-bow or somethin'.*

*You still want to take a look at those stallions, Tessie?*

*Naw. I just want to look at this one.*

The gust of laughter that shook the shoulders of the adults made Blue take a few steps back.

*What do you think of the gray one, Tessie? Think your mom would take to her?*

*She isn't as pretty, but yeah, I like her, too. She's brave! See how she's standin' in front of all the rest, lookin' at us!*

*Yessir, that filly is a spunky one, all right. She'll need a strong hand and patience.*

*Mom's got those, right, Dad?*

*Sure does, Tessie. Well, sir, say we wanted to adopt both those fillies, you got any specials runnin'?*

More laughter and the group at the fence broke apart, some families walking across the road to the stallions' pen, some wandering back to the cars. The low-voiced man and the little girl followed Blue's captors back to the barn. The screen door banged shut behind them, and the dust and the day settled down once more.

. . .

**BLUE'S CHANCE CAME TWO DAYS LATER.**

By now, she and Doe and the other recent captures

were totally familiar with the routine of their new life. The men brought fresh water and hay in the morning, just after sunup. The sun's glare moved predictably across the corral, blazing hot and high at midday, throwing long shadows from the fence line in the evening, when the men brought more water. The mustangs swished flies, stared at the hills beyond. Occasionally one of the men would separate a stallion or a mare from their group and drive them through the chute again for unknown purposes. Sometimes the stallions would call out to the fillies, and Blue remembered the *grullo*, with his sweeping tail and proud young head. She had almost answered him.

It was the smell of rain that did it, finally . . . or perhaps it would have happened anyway. The rain unleashed the unbearable longing that filled Blue's heart, but it had never been far from the surface. She had waited; she had learned. And two evenings after the visitors came, Blue acted.

It was one of the rare all-day thundershowers, when the sky over the corrals turned the colors of Blue's own coat, and the clouds rolled over the far hills much as they had over the mountains of the fillies' home. Usually the rains here were short and sharp, beginning with a crash of thunder and sprays of distant lightning and ending almost as violently as they began, with a washed and brilliant sky framing the sun that would quickly dry the corrals' puddles, baking the hard earth red again. But on this afternoon, the rains were more determined, or more leisurely: The air held its moisture, the sky kept giving more, and the dry, dusty land around the mustangs' prison seemed, for once, almost green.

Many of the horses were miserable in the pens, unused to the soaking they were receiving. But Blue and Doe reveled in their element: Doe actually splashed a bit in one of the puddles that ringed the corral, and Blue ran in lightning-quick bursts along the fence line, Roman head held high up to the clouds, the thunder, the smell of home.

Lou Weatherall (the man who refilled the mustangs' water trough in the evenings) grumbled all the way to the fillies' corral. Any fool could see that there was plenty of water tonight, but his boss insisted that he check the troughs anyway. He trudged across the muddy expanse of the parking lot, his green raincoat flapping in the gusts of wind that drove the rain diagonally across his face. The gate was slick in his grip, and he struggled briefly between the latch and his wide-brimmed black cowboy hat, which the breeze threatened to tear from its snug hold on his brow. Suddenly, the wind won, and Lou felt the hat take flight. He made a grab for it, lost his footing in the slick muck under his boots, and man and hat fell to the ground in an undignified sprawl. More unfortunately for Lou, he lost his grip on the gate, and the wind pushed it wide open, giving Blue, for the first time, a view of the hills beyond . . . with no barrier in between!

She acted before she thought, as if pricked by a live wire. While the other horses huddled grimly under the downpour, preoccupied with their discomfort, Blue dove forward and, with a few bounding strides, was out, past the gate, past the corral, on the other side of the fence, leaping over the fallen cowboy and heading for the hills!

*Crash!* came the thunder. *Crash!* went the flailing gate, banging wide. *Splash!* went Lou Weatherall as he struggled, shouting and cursing, in the mud. Then: *Neigh!* came Doe's cry as her sister, dizzied with the sight of unfenced horizons and with the smell of rain and leaves and green growing things (oh, the honeysuckle on the hills, the snowmelt, the breeze through the tamarack!), struggled to keep her footing as her pinwheeling legs drove her forward to freedom.

*Come on, Doe!* Blue called.

Her sister's return cry was filled with anxiety and confusion.

*Hurry!* Blue trumpeted. Lou Weatherall was almost to his feet. Blue doubled back to the fence, every muscle of her strong, compact body tensed for flight, the rain streaming down her forelock and into her eyes. She tossed her head wildly, encouraging her sister forward.

*Come on, Doe!*

But Doe seemed momentarily frozen. Her rolling eyes flickered between her sister, the man with the rope, and the herd at her side.

*I'm afraid!* she whinnied desperately to Blue, who wheeled back and forth outside the fence, hooves churning mud. Doe looked again to the pinto, to the old mare and her strong foal. The herd watched Blue with interest but did not move to join her. There was safety in numbers. And the man was now blocking the gate.

*They're not our family, Doe! They're not our herd! We have to go home!*

Something in her sister's piercing call—a note of authority, of love, of remembrance of home—broke through Doe's panic and her powerful instinct to stay with the group. Holding Blue's gaze, she bolted forward, springing like a deer toward the gate as Blue reared with joy, cheering her on.

The gate hit Doe in the chest.

Flung awkwardly backward, Doe shrilled with pain and confusion. But Lou Weatherall grimly pressed forward, blocking the mustang's momentum, and with a wrench of wet metal and wood, he secured the gate firmly against the fence post.

*No!* screamed Blue, pawing the mud in a frenzy, wheeling in place, straining to get closer to her sister. Her hooves banged the outside of the corral as Doe's banged the inside. The fence was high, but the sisters could see each other's heads and wide, panic-struck eyes.

*I can't get to you!* Doe called.

All Blue could do was cry out as she turned again, racing the fence line, as if she'd discover another opening, another chance for Doe. . . .

And then, even through the noise of the storm, she heard the whistle of the rope singing past her head and the loud, barking voice of Lou Weatherall at its other end. Blue shied away, spinning on her back legs, and the rope fell harmlessly to her side. But the man soon had it back and began to swing it in the ominous circle around his head. Blue cantered a few strides away, still calling to her sister, torn between fear of capture and the fear of losing sight of Doe, just unreachable, her smell still clear, so close and yet so completely cut off from her!

*Wossshhh!* The rope came closer this time, and Blue had to move fast to skirt the noose.

*Go, Blue! Men are coming!*

Blue turned, following her sister's gaze, and saw two more men, their garments flapping in the wind like strange birds, splashing through the river of mud that was the parking lot, running toward her with ropes in their hands.

*Doe!* she cried in anguish.

*Go!* her sister urged, eyes wide and fearful—and yet they were eyes filled with love.

The second and third ropes slashed through the rain, grazing Blue's hindquarters and hocks. The men shouted angrily. Blue blasted out her defiance, nostrils flared, her rugged head lifted high as she reached skyward with her forelegs, rearing to the top of her height, then plunging forward as the next toss of the ropes again just grazed her neck.

But she knew this wasn't a fight she could win, not if she stayed here by the pen . . . by Doe.

*Go!* Doe pleaded, and now her eyes were gentle and calm. *Go home!*

As the men raised their ropes again, Blue bolted.

She ran for the rain-swept hills. She ran for the unbroken space before her. She ran for home. She ran for her sister, who could not run. And the rain came down, blotting out the hoofprints that were the only trace she left behind.

# CHAPTER 7

**I**T WAS DARK BEFORE BLUE STOPPED RUNNING.
It was dark and the rain had slowed to a fine mist blurring the evening star that glanced out from behind the curtains of clouds. Blue had run blindly from the corral, her only goal to reach the hills that had meant freedom during her weeks in the pen. Now she was at their base and through the last light of the day she could see that they were gentle inclines, studded with rocks and sharp, prickly plants and muddy from the rains. She slowed to a trot, sides heaving from her exertions, mud, sweat, and rain blanketing her coat. Alternating between a fast walk and a jog, she picked her way carefully up the slick slope, her strong legs, sturdy build, and tough hooves keeping her upright and balanced.

Blue didn't stop until she reached the top of the hill, where she finally let herself slow to a halt and surveyed the strange scene spread out in the valley below her.

It looked as if the stars had fallen from the night

sky: Above, the clouds formed an unbroken curtain of darkness, and below, a thousand brightly colored flares twinkled in the foothills. To her left, a river of light seemed to snake around the dazzling field. Occasionally, moving lights streamed down the river. The field itself was composed of multicolored stars, some that flickered and others that were still. It stretched out as far as her eye could see to the right, but Blue could make out darkness on the other side of the light river. After several moments of indecision, she decided to head for that patch of night beyond this spectacle of fallen stars.

It was trickier going down the hill than it had been going up. The footing was slicker and the brightness below made it difficult for Blue to pick out a trail before her. Reluctantly, she slowed her pace. Tiredness began to steal through her, but she never stumbled. In this strange land, she was on full alert, tired or not. And focusing intently on the task ahead prevented her from thinking about what she had left behind.

After a few hours of steady slogging, the land under her hooves evened out and became easier to navigate. She was down the hill and level with the lights. Blue stopped and sniffed the air. She could smell rain and mud but also another familiar yet ominous scent: men's trucks. Blue tossed her head, trying to determine the direction of the smell, but it was too diffuse. She pawed the ground briefly, uncertain what to do. It seemed as if the acrid odor was stronger toward the light river, but it came from the light field as well. Now that she was even with both, it was harder to tell which direction might be safer. Blue remembered her father standing atop the high crest of a hill on their home range, surveying the land for predators. It was better to be up high, but unless she wanted to turn around, back toward the corrals, Blue had no choice but to press forward into the unknown.

She scraped the earth a few more times with the tip of a hoof and headed left toward the darkness beyond the highway.

. . .

WITH A ROAR AND A BLAST OF FOUL-SMELLING wind, a huge truck hurtled past Blue and she swerved left, fear adding more speed to her stride. When she'd discovered that what had looked like a river from afar was actually where the men's trucks roamed, and roamed at speeds she could barely fathom, she'd had two choices: to go back, or to try to go around the highway. The trucks seemed to catapult out of the darkness like boulders falling during an avalanche, and their brilliant lights blinded her just as the blast of their horns pierced her ears and the weight of their stride shook the very ground beneath her hooves. All of Blue's instincts told her to get as far away from this place as possible, but the filly refused to retreat. Now she had stumbled through several miles of scrub brush, ditches, and woods, trying to find the highway's end, and she was exhausted, tense, and confused. A conflict raged within her: She could feel that the direction of home lay on the other side of the terrifying road, and she knew for a fact that the corrals lay behind her, but the highway seemed never to end! Even worse: The farther she struggled through the woods on the side of the road, the closer she seemed to get to even more lights. And lights, she was now certain, meant danger. Blue decided that she had to cross the highway.

It took several tries before Blue could command her unwilling body to move forward into the road, but eventually she forced herself halfway across, on the grassy strip of land that divided the east- and westbound lanes. Now there were trucks on either side of her: Some came at her from the front and others from behind! The comforting darkness she had seen from the hill should be to her left, but her view of it was blocked by a wall—not as high as the corral's fence but solid. Each time a truck zoomed by, Blue panicked and kept running straight ahead, down the median, her ability to think scrambled by the noise and the lights and the hot fumy blasts of wind that the monsters left in their wake.

Finally, the highway was momentarily quiet. Blue halted abruptly, limbs trembling. Behind her, she could see a distant glimmer of approaching headlights, but ahead the only light was the faint blush of dawn. Blue snorted, tossed her now dry and matted mane, and took a long, appraising look at the wall before her. She had jumped higher barriers, but not without having an idea of what was on the other side.

She glanced backward: The approaching lights were growing brighter, and her sensitive hooves could feel a low tremor in the earth. She had to make her move before the next herd of trucks came on.

Blue took a few steps backward and shook her forelock from her eyes. Her body tensed, preparing for flight. She briefly pawed the grass of the median and gave a half rear. And then she was off: leaping forward, hooves meeting the hard asphalt with a clatter as she bounded in a few powerful strides across the road and flung herself up, up, and over the gray concrete wall.

Her forelegs hit the tangled briars first, then the rest of Blue's weight landed awkwardly on the steep slope beyond the wall. Her right foreleg buckled beneath her, sending her head and neck down to receive their share of scratches from the thorny mess into which she'd leaped. Blue struggled upright, planting her legs firmly to stop her forward momentum. But she only stayed still for a moment: The sharp branches of the roadside scrub made it too uncomfortable to linger. Blue shuddered: Her coat was laced with nicks and stinging welts and she was surrounded by vegetation that seemed to trap her. She had no choice but to plunge ahead, down the slope, into the blackness.

. . .

IT WAS AN UNCOMFORTABLE TWENTY MINUTES before Blue was out of the thicket. When she finally stumbled through the last of the brambles and paused to take her bearings, the morning's first light was bringing out the faint gray outlines of the landscape around her. A thicket of small but densely planted trees blocked the view directly ahead, but Blue thought she saw the first of the sun's rays peeping through the grove. The smell of fumes still bedeviled her nostrils; she hoped she'd left the worst of it behind. Bracing herself, Blue trotted forward through a slight break in the trees, toward the light.

Her hooves hit the pavement at almost the same moment that a trucker jumped down from his rig, eager to stretch his legs and order some breakfast. Blue skidded back on her haunches, for a confused moment convinced that she was back at Ezra Ryder's—but no . . . same bright light, a false sun hovering high in the sky, same gathering of trucks, same searing smell of gasoline and exhaust, but no corral, no pine trees . . . as Blue turned frantically to the left and right, all she could see was more road, more gray buildings with a few lights twinkling on.

The trucker spat out his last mouthful of cold coffee as the filly emerged like a gray ghost from the thicket. But he only had a moment to take in the strange sight of the wild Appaloosa lost in the parking lot of the Chief Joseph Truck Stop. As he watched the small, rain-colored filly turn several circles, hooves sliding out beneath her on the slick asphalt, the trucker's arms broke out in goose bumps. This was no stray pony, he realized. This was a visitor from another century . . . from a country that no longer existed. The wild horse circled once more, then broke to the left, heading north out of the parking lot and onto the service road. The trucker watched her go, still not entirely sure if he could believe his eyes.

. . .

**THE BLAST OF A HORN DROVE BLUE OFF THE** road and into another parking lot. The sound of her hooves on the hard pavement was like hail on stones as she galloped across the meadow of concrete that fronted the row of big box stores that were just turning on their lights in preparation for opening. She jumped a hedge that divided one strip of stores from the next and almost collided with a girl getting out of her car to start her shift at the coffeehouse. Blue swerved, nicking the car, and bounded past the store's neon-lighted window as startled early-morning patrons stared, as unsure as the trucker had been of what they were seeing.

As she galloped away from the coffee shop, Blue heard the sound of engines behind her. She gave a burst of speed, maneuvering past telephone poles and the parking lot's lights, employees' cars, and concrete planters filled with marigolds. With a throaty roar, the trucks gave chase. For a moment, Blue thought their shared path was a mistake—that the trucks would drop back to the station where they seemed to gather, or go run on the road. But after she leaped another planter, moving farther into the interior of the lot, toward the storefronts, she realized that the trucks were, in fact, following *her*. Soon they were close enough that she could hear the loud, exuberant voices of the men inside them. She swiveled her eyes to look behind her: Two men seemed to be riding the back of one truck, outside its body. It only took another glance to see that one of these men was twirling a rope over his head, and it only took another moment before Blue bolted with all the speed she could muster, cutting recklessly across the path of the second truck and charging back toward the road.

With what seemed a shriek of pain, the second truck swerved violently to the right, its back end fishtailing. Blue didn't pause to look behind her: The sound of crashing metal and the sudden silence of the engines told her enough, as did the men's furious voices.

In Blue's experience, when men sounded that way, she was winning.

But it wasn't many miles later that Blue began to despair that her victory was short-lived, that in the new world she'd entered since her capture, there was no avoiding the handiwork of men.

While at first glance the land that stretched before her after she'd left behind the last of the shopping mall appeared unmarked, in reality its contours were shaped by yet more fences, by roads—dirt and paved and graveled—and by buildings. So far, these had been sparse, and Blue hadn't seen any actual men, but she met more of their captive animals—large, horned creatures, docile and slow moving—grazing in the greener fields, which were almost always barricaded in some way. By midday, Blue had jumped barbed-wire fences, hunted out and crossed over broken fence lines, and stolen water from the cows' troughs. She was growing tired and hot, plagued by horseflies and gnats that swarmed over her torn coat.

But eventually, she became aware that the land around her *was* changing—and changing dramatically. As the miles and the hours passed, the dusty, low, rolling hills became steeper and forested, and the intermittently grassy fields grew greener with a variety of living plants. As the signs of men grew fainter, Blue's spirits lifted further, and a renewed sense of purpose animated her stride.

Mostly what she felt was space: It was as if there was suddenly more air. As she walked, she drank in the breeze, relishing the scent of scrub plants, drying earth, and, for the first time since the corral, other wild animals. She was sure there were a few deer nearby, perhaps some groundhogs. Tired, dirty, and sore as she was, a feeling of well-being stole through her as if borne on the rays of the setting sun. Her heart ached for Doe; yet, too, her heart ached for home . . . and she was going home. She was going home! The welts on her back, her bruised hooves, her exhausted body: These seemed to fall away as Blue contemplated the unbroken space before her—miles of it, harsh and unknown—but unfenced. After another deep, sustaining breath of the fresh air, the Appaloosa continued north.

# CHAPTER 8

WHEN BLUE OPENED HER EYES THE NEXT morning, she thought she must still be dreaming. She had slept heavier than she'd meant to, her cautiousness for once overwhelmed by exhaustion. But no harm had come to her here, in this place she now gazed at with wondering eyes. She had followed the scent of water until she reached a small creek, shrouded in darkness, the night before. After drinking deeply, the filly had actually lain down and fallen asleep—something she hadn't done since she was a foal, not counting the miserable period of unconsciousness in the trailer. Lulled by the soft, burbling voice of the stream, Blue had slept and dreamed of home. Doe was there, and Shadow, too. Shadow and Fly were playing, and Doe was by her side, watching them. Their father and Blue's mother were nearby, grazing peacefully under the warm summer sunshine. Above, Blue could hear the voice of a hawk calling to his mate. . . . It was so loud . . . the hawk must be close by. . . .

Blue awoke, the wild, free cry still echoing in her ears. There it was again! Blue raised her muzzle to the branches above, searching the trees for her dream bird. And just as she realized she was awake, she saw him: With a flash of white throat and belly and the swoop of a dark wing, the hawk launched from his nearby nest and swept up and out into the morning sky.

With a grunt, Blue braced her forelegs and clambered to her feet. She gave a few good shakes, setting dust motes and flakes of dried mud loose from her coat. Slowly, she made her way over to the creek bed and bent her head to drink. The cold, fresh water was almost a shock as it poured down her throat, so different it was from the warm, stale buckets she'd drunk from for so many weeks. Blue drank and drank, savoring the taste of home in every mouthful. When her thirst was quenched, she splashed a little in the stream from sheer rising spirits, and then it occurred to her that if the water here was this good, what must the grass be like?

The previous night had been moonless and cloudy, so Blue's sense of the land through which she'd traveled was mostly of its smell and outline, and of the quiet that lay over the hills. The night air was cool and smelled of flowers and ponderosa pines and living creatures. Blue hadn't paused to eat after the sun set. She had simply walked, following her inner course north and east until she caught the scent of water and finally rested. Now the Appaloosa was curious to see her surroundings in the light of day. She bounded a bit stiffly out of the stream and trotted with purpose to the opening in the stands of willow trees whose long, graceful branches made a protective curtain around the sun-dappled glade where she'd spent the night.

For a horse that had spent weeks in the world of men, the meadow that stretched before the dazzled filly was like another continuation of her dream of home. Oh, she had longed for space, and here was *space*! The bunchgrass prairie stretched out as far as Blue's eyes could see, peppered with paintbrush and the bright wildflowers of high summer. The stream where she'd watered continued northeast, edged by pine trees teeming with sparrows and squirrels. The morning sky was blazing blue, the creek burbled merrily behind her, the meadow's tall green and dun-colored grasses swayed in the breeze. The tired filly ran out to meet it all. She ran out to freedom.

As she cantered into the sunshine, Blue couldn't help but feel that there was something familiar about this land. Of course the absence of men and the presence of unfenced space reminded her of home, but the rolling prairie was very different from the mountains that sheltered her family. Yet her spirit responded to these verdant, life-filled fields as if she were returning to a beloved place, half remembered, perhaps visited only in a dream. . . .

After a long, luxurious graze and another drink from the creek, Blue was ready to move on. The sun was climbing the sky, the day was growing hotter, and the filly didn't know how far she still had to travel or where this path would lead. But for the moment, the path itself was almost as good as home.

. . .

A FEW HOURS LATER, BLUE FOUND HERSELF AT the foothills of a series of buttes rising from the prairie. She didn't stop to graze or to make a sidetrack for water: A view was exactly what she needed most. She swung into a jog and headed up the slope, eager to see what was on the other side and to take stock of the road ahead. While she hadn't encountered any animals larger or more frightening than a mule deer, Blue knew that she shouldn't let her guard down. And like her father, she did her best thinking with a long range to contemplate.

But nothing could have prepared Blue for what she found when she reached the top of the butte.

The prairie continued to stretch out before her, as rich and inviting as the fields through which she'd just traveled, but now Blue could also see a soaring line of white-tipped mountains that plunged down into canyons just visible to the east. The land seemed to undulate before her eyes, as dynamic as a rushing river: flowers and grass, forest and glade, mountain and rock! Snow and sun, sparrow and hawk! Stream and river, prairie and butte, deer and . . . *horse!*

The scent hit her nostrils just as Blue threw up her head, and she skidded to a halt. Her eyes followed the breeze's direction down and to the east, and there, sure enough, loping along the line of trees that Blue guessed edged another stream, appeared two horselike figures . . . but what was on their backs? Blue stared in confusion, trying to make sense of the ropes looping about the horses' heads and the strange forms that rose behind their withers. And then another all-too-familiar smell hit her: men!

Her mind reeling, Blue turned circles atop the crest of the butte, every movement speaking her amazement. She tossed her head frantically and pawed the earth. A neigh rose and died in her throat. What could this mean? How were the men and horses combined? Finally, her frustration and fear broke through and Blue screamed a high, wild note that echoed over the valley like the cry of an eagle. She screamed again, raising her forelegs to scratch at the sky and to show her defiance of the bizarre creatures below. She would not show her fear. Like her father, she would announce her presence and expect to be heeded!

Heeded she was: At the sound of her piercing whistle, the two quarter horses froze in their tracks. Their startled riders looked for the source of the eerie noise and were almost as surprised by the sight of the small gray filly rearing her full height at the top of the butte as Blue had been surprised by them.

*Someone's got a loose horse.*

*A loose crazy horse, from the looks of it.*

*Let's go check it out.*

The quarter horses needed little encouragement to start up the hill: They were straining with eagerness to inspect the strange horse, and they bounded forward, ears pricked and eyes alight with curiosity.

Blue could hardly believe it. Instead of yielding, the horses and men were coming straight for her! She took a few steps back and shrieked again but still they came on. Now she could see them in more detail: The lead horse was at least two hands taller than Blue, well fed, with a glossy chestnut coat and a white blaze that gave his face an open, friendly expression. A smaller palomino mare followed; she, too, appeared unfazed by Blue's threatening signals. Both horses moved easily under the men on their backs—men who were *riding* them . . . using them like their trucks!

*It's an Appaloosa! Don't the Indians still breed them?*

*Sure, but in Idaho. Kinda far for her to travel . . . and across Hell's Canyon, no less.*

*I don't suppose you protect any wild horses on the preserve?*

*Wish we did, especially if they were like this one. But I expect she's some rancher's half-broke runaway. I'll make a few calls when we get back.*

*Hang on—is that a brand on her neck? See there, just under her mane?*

*Let's try to get a little closer.*

As the horses and men again moved toward her, Blue bolted. She could hear a plaintive whinny of disappointment from the friendly chestnut, but she didn't care. She didn't care who these horses were or where they came from. They were from the world of men and that was all the filly felt she needed to know. Here, in this beautiful place that had felt like home, there were still men. And even worse, there were men *on* horses!

Blue no longer paused to graze or to water or to enjoy the view. Though the horse-men didn't pursue her, nor did she encounter any more of them down the trail, she did see cows, and where these placid creatures were, Blue had learned, there were men nearby. Her heart hammered in her chest as she galloped over the prairie, slowing to a jog to catch her wind, then powering forward when panic struck again. Soon her fears were confirmed: fences ahead! A building! A road! The building was distant and the narrow dirt road was empty, but Blue was taking no chances. Legs churning beneath her, the Appaloosa plunged toward the forest that edged the canyon she'd seen from the butte.

When she slipped among the forest's protective branches, a dappled shadow amid shadows, the tired filly finally rested. Unlike most horses, Blue was used to the woods and used to finding shelter in them. She had even, she remembered now with a pang, found Doe in them.

Blue did not pause for long: The urge to put more distance between herself and the men was too strong.

Soon she was picking her way through the ponderosas and down the rocky hillside. Blue tread warily: The slope was growing steeper and she had caught a glimpse of what looked like a snake warming itself in the late-afternoon sun. But she could see the river below, a narrow band of gleaming blue, and knew she would feel more at ease once she reached the other side.

. . .

**THE SUN WAS SETTING AS BLUE CLIMBED THE** last few steps up to the top of the craggy ridge. Behind her, the quiet bend of the Imnaha River reflected the sky's copper and salmon glow. Before her, shrouded in the blue twilit shadow of the promontory on which she stood, wound the Snake River, twice as wide as the Imnaha and banked by rock-strewn canyons. It was going to be a hazardous descent, especially as the sky lost light, but Blue was a filly of the mountains, tough and sure-footed, and she was confident in her ability to navigate rough terrain. She started down the trail, toward the sound of rushing water below.

Suddenly, a shape loomed out from a shadowed crevice just ahead of her. Blue paused mid-step, her nerves tautening as she peered wide-eyed into the gloom of the rock formations. Softly, she sniffed the air, but the thing was downwind. She carefully lowered her hoof, trying not to make a sound. There could be cougars here, or bobcats . . . or men. The shape was a darker shadow against shadows and appeared to be crouching. It wasn't bothering to conceal its presence, either: Blue could hear it tap-tapping along the rocks. The filly took a tentative step backward, wondering if she could find another route to the riverbed. And then: *BAAAAA!* An incredible noise that must have come from the creature echoed through the canyon. It rang again, even more insistently: *BAAAAAAAA!* The sound of Blue's clattering hooves as she spooked was drowned out by the answering chorus: *BA! BAA! BA!* A whole pack of the horned, woolly beasts now emerged from the twilight, braying their heads off. As they drew nearer, Blue could see that the animals had hooves and were much smaller than she. They were also, she thought as her breathing returned to its normal rate, exceptionally silly looking. Feeling silly herself, the mustang snorted haughtily at the sheep and resumed her trek down the canyon.

Moonlight painted the river silver and cast the surrounding sandy banks in a soft, dreamlike glow. The canyon was filled with the sound of the river as it rushed north. Upstream, Blue could just make out the froth of white foam where the water met rock, but this bend appeared calm. Still, she could not gauge how deep or how fast the river ran, nor what was beyond the curve downstream, at least not from her perch on the banks. It would be safer to wait until sunup to attempt the crossing, Blue knew, but she was unnerved by this forbidding land. It was a place of stones and treacherous pathways, strange creatures and plunging cliffs. It had taken all of the sense and care the hardy filly could muster to pick her way safely to the canyon floor, and she was not at all certain that all of the eyes that gleamed at her from the darkness belonged to sheep. She shuddered when an eagle screamed from a nearby pine; this was not a riverbank where she wanted to linger.

The water that flowed around her fetlocks as she took her first tentative step into the Snake was bracingly cold. Blue went a few more strides in—so far, the current seemed calm. The mustang had never swum this distance before, but she and her sister liked to paddle in the narrow, but deep, stream at home. Thinking of Doe, Blue steeled herself and plunged forward toward the heart of the river.

By the time the water was to her shoulder, Blue's hooves were dragged out from under her and she was sucked downstream so forcefully, it was as if she had been struck by the eye of a hurricane. She was spun violently around, now swept hindquarters first by the sickeningly strong current. Struggling to keep her muzzle above the roiling water, the Appaloosa desperately tried to get her legs coordinated beneath her to swim, to struggle, to do anything to stop this mad catapult in the current's grip.

It was no use: No matter how hard she pumped her legs, she was powerless against the river's strength. She was turned helplessly around and around as if she were no bigger than Shadow, and as she spun, her body collided with rocks and bracken lodged in the riverbed. Nothing seemed able to stop her painful plunge, but still Blue fought desperately. She fought for her life.

Suddenly, the river's roar grew even louder and Blue caught a glimpse of something large and white looming ahead in the moonlight. Then her head went under. *Crack.* Her left hind leg smashed against a hidden boulder. Blue frantically tried to get her head up, but she had been thrown on her side and couldn't right herself. *Smack.* Her poll smacked a rock, shooting stars before her eyes.

*It's over*, Blue thought through the dizzy clouds that filled her head. *I can't make it.* And the battered filly let her body grow slack as she and the river rushed inexorably toward the rapids.

Perhaps it was the cessation of her movement that did it—Blue never knew—but like a storm-tossed boat that finds its way to shore, the mustang's hooves suddenly scraped sand. She moved her forelegs feebly, and again they dragged against the bottom! She was instantly awake, alive . . . there was solid ground beneath her and she was going to make it, if only she could find the strength to battle the current one last time. With all of the force of her passionate, free heart, and all of the power of her small, tough body, the Appaloosa lunged toward the riverbank and pulled herself out.

# CHAPTER 9

JOE SAW THE APPALOOSA FIRST.

It was his favorite day of the week (Saturday, when his grandfather drove up to Moscow to pick Joe up and take him back to the reservation to spend the weekend); he was in his favorite place (the hot vinyl seat of his grandfather's ancient pickup truck); and they were on their way to do one of his favorite things (fishing). Plus, his grandfather was taking him to a new spot, one that was only accessible by a rough dirt road that wound over the Joseph Plains, over creeks and knolls that jounced and jostled the rusty truck and threw grandfather and grandson into fits of gleeful laughter.

"It's like riding a bronc!" Joe gasped as they hauled out of another rocky creek bed.

"If we don't make it, can you push the truck back? I'm too old." His grandfather, Sam Gray Wolf, chuckled. "You're ten now, big and strong."

"Sure, Grandpa. Or I could carry you to Great-uncle

Josiah's ranch on my back, like one of his horses." Sam Gray Wolf's brother bred horses on a small ranch just north of the new fishing spot—it had been Josiah who'd suggested it—and they were supposed to bring back their catch for dinner with him and his wife, Joe's great-aunt Mary.

"I hope my crazy brother knows what he's talking about," Sam muttered as the truck lurched wildly left, pitching Joe practically into his grandfather's lap. "This spot better have fish jumping onto the banks."

"That would be nice," Joe sighed. He hadn't caught a thing their last two trips. He grabbed hold of the strap hanging from the truck's ceiling, bracing himself for the next hill, and peered through the dirt- and fly-specked windshield at the overcast summer day. A great day for fishing, or so his grandfather said. Sam insisted that fish didn't like to see their shadows. Joe glanced over at him and couldn't help smiling—his grandfather always stuck the tip of his tongue out of the corner of his mouth when he was concentrating, and Joe saw it peeking out now as Sam steered with a death grip on the wheel.

When he looked forward again, Joe saw her. At first he wasn't sure what exactly it was he was seeing—something gray and dappled slipping into the trees . . . too big to be a deer. . . .

"Grandpa, stop the truck for a second." Joe stuck his head out the window to get a better look.

"I may never get it started again," Sam grumbled. "You can't wait till we get there?"

"No, it's not that. I thought I saw something going into the woods. Like a horse."

"Now, *that* would be unusual," Sam replied, and he braked so suddenly that Joe's forehead nearly smacked the windshield. "Sorry, Joey." His grandfather grinned ruefully. "But it *would* be unusual. And interesting."

Grandfather and grandson hopped out of the truck simultaneously, and the curiosity that lit their faces made them look like older and younger versions of the same person, though Sam wore his hair in a long single braid and Joe had his cropped short. Sam had also put on a few pounds around the middle with age, and Joe, though not especially tall for his age, was wiry.

To Blue, their similarities or differences hardly mattered. She had tried to escape into the trees when she heard the truck coming, but now she knew it was useless. They were pursuing her on foot, and she couldn't outrun them. Not this time. Though she could not flee, the filly could at least face her enemy. Slowly, she hobbled around and raised her battered head high in defiance.

As they drew nearer, Sam gave a low whistle.

"Grandpa, what happened to her?" Joe stared at the bruised and bloodied horse in dismay.

"I have no idea. But I think we'll have to save the fish for another day, Joey. We've got to get this horse some help."

. . .

**THE VOICES FILTERED IN AND OUT OF BLUE'S** consciousness.

*She's a Bureau horse. . . . Reckon someone adopted her and she escaped? . . . Probably should call the folks in Moscow . . . Funny that we found her so close to the crossing . . . She looks like one of the old ones, doesn't she?*

The stall was cool and comfortable with a fan blowing a gentle breeze through the high window. Blue stood, head drooping, half in a dream. There had been more ropes and another trailer, but it was not as frightening as it had been the first time. Now she was actually in one of the men's buildings, but surrounded by the scent of her own kind. There were other good smells, too, borne on the breeze: grass and trees and water. Blue sighed in her half doze and listened.

*She looks like she's been beaten up pretty bad. Whoever had her doesn't deserve to get her back, that's for darn sure.*

*No*, Blue thought, *I should* not *go back to the river.* And then suddenly, she startled awake, snorting with surprise. She had understood the men's words!

"Hah, she's awake," Josiah said, switching back to English from the Nez Perce tongue in which he and his brother had been speaking, as they often did together. "It's incredible that she doesn't have more serious injuries. When I first saw her, I thought she was much worse off than she is."

"She's a survivor, that's certain," Sam said thoughtfully. And Blue, hearing the voices return to an incomprehensible murmur, went back to sleep.

. . .

**THE BOY WAS STANDING OUTSIDE HER STALL,** peering at her through the bars. Blue backed automatically into the far corner and stared back at him. He had the same sweetish odor as the children who had visited the corral—it wasn't as unpleasant as men usually smelled. The boy slowly put his hand through the bars and opened his palm. He was holding something out, Blue didn't know what. She eased back a bit farther into the stall and blew a warning note through her nostrils.

The boy held his position for a long time, talking in a soft stream, but finally he made a face, dropped the thing into the sawdust, and left the barn.

Some time later, Blue took a cautious step toward the object the boy had left behind. It looked like a short, chubby stick, but it smelled delicious. Blue nosed it, then startled back as dramatically as if she'd been struck by a snake when it rolled over beneath her breath. A few minutes later, courage regained, Blue nosed the thing again. It smelled so good! She put her lips against it and gave it a brief lick. That did it: Throwing caution to the wind, the filly gobbled up the carrot, relishing the sweet, crisp, unfamiliar taste. It was so *good*! Blue looked around the stall on the off chance that the boy had dropped more of these wonderful things, but no luck. And despite herself, Blue found that she wouldn't mind if he happened to come back. As long as he kept his distance . . . and brought carrots.

. . .

**THE OLD MEN DIDN'T KEEP THEIR DISTANCE,** but Blue, hobbled by her sore body, was unable to fend off their ministrations. Day after day, they put their hands on her, leaving behind the sharp smell of herbs. While she was in the trailer, they had put something around her head that allowed them to hold it still and to tie her to the sides of the stall. Too tired and injured to protest, the filly became accustomed to their regular visits as well as to those of the boy, who had since broadened Blue's treat repertoire to include apples and sugar cubes. She would only eat them from the floor of the stall, never from his hand, and he had to back all the way to the barn's entrance before she'd approach the offering, but Joe was still proud of his progress. At least she wouldn't refuse to eat them until he was out of sight!

For Joe and his grandfather and great-uncle, trying to solve the riddle of what had happened to the mysterious Appaloosa was even better than reading a detective novel. First Josiah had contacted the Bureau of Land Management offices in Boise, but they had no record of housing a blue roan Appaloosa filly—or of any Appaloosa, for that matter—during the past year. The woman at the Boise office told Josiah to check the filly's freezemark, and when he read her back the registration number branded under Blue's mane, she told Josiah that the Appaloosa had been penned in Oregon, not Idaho. This set off another round of calls: Josiah and Sam to the BLM offices; Sam to Joe, back in Moscow, reporting on the brothers' progress; Joe to Josiah, wondering when he could come back to the ranch to see the filly; the BLM offices to Josiah, apologizing for the delay and asking for his patience; Sam to his daughter, Joe's mother, asking if Joe could spend a week with him and Josiah and Mary on the ranch; and Joe to Sam, at midnight, too excited about his upcoming visit to sleep!

It was over pancakes in Mary's kitchen the morning after he arrived that the phone call came.

"Mr. Gray Wolf? This is the Oregon BLM office calling. I heard y'all found our runaway."

"Runaway, huh?" Josiah raised his eyebrows in surprise. Joe and Sam started clamoring for more details and he raised a hand to shush them so he could hear.

"Yessir, she broke out of one of our adoption facilities a coupla weeks ago, over near Enterprise. Where y'all at? We'll send someone to come and get her."

"Not real close to Enterprise is where we're at." Josiah laughed. "Your filly's crossed state lines into Idaho."

"Back where we picked her up—ain't that a funny thing?" The man sounded bemused.

"How'd you mean?" Josiah's face registered such surprise this time that Joe and Sam demanded an explanation and he had to ask the BLM man to hang on while he caught them up.

"Apparently, some cowboys found her and another Appaloosa up in the Selway-Bitterroot Wilderness, or somewhere thereabouts. Old guy had stopped them— thought they were gonna sell 'em to a slaughterhouse, and maybe they were. . . . He had the fillies corralled back of his gas station, and he called us. I was bringing some other horses to Enterprise and I swung by and got 'em."

"So you don't know where the cowboys found her?"

"Well, pretty close to that gas station, I b'lieve. I think that old man knew a bit more than he was letting on, as a matter of fact. Anyway, she's a Bureau horse now."

"Hmm. You remember his name?"

"I got it here somewhere. . . . Gimme a sec . . . uh, Ryder. Ezra Ryder."

"Ryder. Ezra Ryder," Josiah repeated, looking at Sam with a twinkle in his eye. "Thanks very much for your help. I 'preciate it."

"Wait a minute now—you haven't told me where you got the filly. We gotta make arrangements—"

"Thanks again. I'll be talking with you," Josiah said briskly and hung up. He looked at his brother and started to laugh.

"Ezra Ryder," Sam said, mystified. "What's that coot got to do with this?"

. . .

**THE BOY WAS BACK AGAIN, AND THIS TIME IT** appeared he wasn't going to drop the carrot. He'd had his arm stuck through the bars for about half an hour, trying to coax her near. Stubbornly, Blue stayed stock-still in the corner of her stall. Just as stubbornly, the boy kept the carrot dangling tantalizingly near . . . but still in his hand.

One of the old men approached, laughing.

"Still won't take it from you, huh?"

"Nope," Joe sighed, disappointed, and withdrew his hand. "I think my arm's fallen asleep."

"Be patient, Joey. She's a wild creature, and I don't think her experience with people has been all that pleasant so far. Tell you what—Josiah's about to take her for another walk, stretch her legs, see how well she's moving. We'll tag along and watch."

Blue and Josiah had taken several of these excursions. The gentle horseman managed to persuade the filly to move beside him without too much resistance. Joe was amazed by his great-uncle's skill with the horse, but Josiah modestly insisted that if Blue were feeling well, he'd have no chance at holding her.

"Look at those eyes! If she had the energy to run, I couldn't stop her, that's for sure. This filly's got the spirit of her ancestors."

"So do you, brother," Sam said, winking. "Our ancestors were horse breeders—*Appaloosa* breeders. I think that's why you two get along."

His quiet younger brother blushed under his deeply tan skin and turned away to tend to the filly standing calmly beside him.

As he watched them, bright eyes flicking from brother to brother, Joe thought how much he wanted to be like his great-uncle and like his grandfather, too. A great horseman and a great fisherman! After all, he was a Gray Wolf, too!

. . .

THAT EVENING, SAM CALLED A FAMILY CONference around the kitchen table.

"I don't want to run things in your own house, Josiah, but I just got off the phone with Ezra, and we have some things to discuss about our filly." Joe hopped up to pour a cup of the strong black coffee that Great-aunt Mary had made. It was bitter and scalding, but it made him feel very grown-up to get to drink a small cup . . . especially since his mother would never have let him.

"Then let's discuss them." Josiah smiled. "How's old Ezra doing anyway?"

"If he's 'old Ezra,' then I'm 'old Sam,'" his brother grumbled. "Our mothers had us on the same day." He turned to Joe. "Ezra Penahwenonmi Ryder is sort of a cousin of ours. . . . We've never figured out exactly how. Our mamas were good friends and we grew up together. He lives off of Highway Twelve, runs a gas station," Sam explained.

"What does Penahwenonmi mean?" Joe asked. He knew some of his tribe's language, but his mother and father didn't speak it, so mostly what he picked up was from his grandfather and great-uncle.

"It means 'helping another,'" Josiah said. "It's an old name. Almost as old as Sam." He winked solemnly at Joe as his brother began to splutter again.

"And he knows about the filly?" Joe pressed on.

"According to Ezra, they got a herd of wild Appaloosa mustangs up where he lives," Sam replied, and his eyes were as bright with excitement as his grandson's.

Josiah grunted with surprise and took a long pull on his pipe. He and his brother looked at each other.

"Wow," Joe said. "Wild horses up in the Wilderness?"

"Wow is right," Josiah said thoughtfully. "And your

grandfather, who likes a good story, thinks that these horses are descendants from the Flight, am I right?"

"Just because it's a good story doesn't mean it's not possible," Sam said defensively. "The way Ezra describes it, there's a whole herd of Appaloosas up there—has been since *his* grandfather's time, so since you think he's so old, that should tell you something."

"Sure does—tells me I'm right!" Josiah laughed, and Sam couldn't help joining in.

"Wait, you mean *our* Flight, the *Nimi'ipuu*?" Joe asked eagerly, trying to keep up.

Josiah nodded. "That's right, Joe. You know the story. Why don't you remind your grandfather of the details?"

Joe knew full well that Grandfather Sam Gray Wolf did not need a lesson in the history of the Nimi'ipuu, or the Nez Perce as they were commonly known—after all, he was the one who had told the boy most of the stories he knew about his ancestors. But Great-uncle Josiah was giving him a chance to contribute to the conversation, and that made him happy. He reached back into his memory, hoping not to disappoint his elders.

"Well, a long time ago, in, like, the eighteen hundreds, Chief Joseph led our people on a long march to get away from the white man's army." He paused.

"That's right," Josiah said encouragingly. "And why did our leader, Chief Joseph, have to do this?"

"Because he didn't want his people to be put in a reservation like the other Nimi'ipuu," Joe said promptly. He hoped Josiah wouldn't ask why the other tribes were already in the reservation, because he couldn't remember. Luckily, his grandfather, unable to stay out of any storytelling, even if he was supposed to be playing student, stepped in.

"Some tribes had already taken the bad deal the U.S. Government had offered them . . . which amounted to giving up most of their land and getting shuffled off to a little old reservation . . . the same little old reservation where you come and visit me."

The lines that spread around Josiah's eyes and down his cheeks, like the tributaries of a river, deepened with sorrow.

"Our fathers' land once spread for thousands and thousands of miles, Joe," he said. "In Oregon and Washington, as well as here in Idaho. Chief Joseph and the other brave leaders like Looking Glass took seven hundred of our people east and north, looking for a new homeland. The army stopped them."

"But they gave them a good chase, didn't they, Greatuncle?" Joe said wistfully.

But it was Sam who answered, his voice ringing with pride. "You bet they did. Matter of fact, it was one of the most brilliant retreats in all military history. And our horses helped us every step of the way."

"So our filly might just have just retraced her steps from the old homeland to the new. . . . Joe, you found her near the place our people—and horses—crossed the Snake River during the Flight," Great-uncle Josiah said.

"The Snake sure could have caused those injuries, too, if she missed the calm spot and got caught in one of the rapids," Sam mused.

Josiah suddenly stood up and pushed his chair back from the table. "Before we continue this discussion, I need to think a bit. Let's all get a good night's sleep and have some dreams and talk in the morning." And with that, Great-uncle Josiah moved abruptly to the kitchen's screen door, shutting it gently behind him.

"'Good night's sleep,' ha," Sam grunted. "I know where he's going. He's going to go talk to that horse."

# CHAPTER 10

BLUE WAS SURPRISED WHEN THE MAN pulled back her stall door—he had never visited her so late before. She was even more surprised when he attached the lead rope, which she'd learned meant they were going out. Sure enough, *Let's have a walk*, he told her, and again she understood the sense of the words. *All right*, she thought. The night air smelled sweet coming through the barn door, and she was a bit restless. Josiah could feel her energy beginning to quicken and knew it meant the filly was healing. He looked at her with satisfaction and stroked her neck. Blue shivered under the caress—it was pleasant, but still strange. She allowed him to do it once more, then pulled back her head sharply. *Enough*. The man removed his hand, and Blue followed him willingly into the soft, star-sprinkled night.

The man didn't seem to be leading her anywhere in particular. They simply ambled, side by side, over the lush green summer grass. He lit a pipe, and Blue bent her head to graze. And as she settled into the deep comfort of walking and nibbling, resting and nibbling, then walking and nibbling again, the man began to talk. Blue listened, but it was listening in a way that was more like feeling than hearing words. Something ancient in her blood was stirred, responding to him, to his smell, his voice, even his touch. And as he told her the story, she realized it was *her* story he was telling. Her story—and his.

*You and me, we've been friends a very long time, though you don't know it,* Josiah Gray Wolf began. *My people, the Nimi'ipuu, helped you come to be. We bred horses with the most beautiful colors and patterns, horses like you—Appaloosas. But we bred for strength, too, just as you are strong and sure of foot. Together, your ancestors and mine ran with the buffalo. . . . Ah, so many years ago. There are no buffalo now.*

*Together, your ancestors and mine traveled to rivers full of salmon for fishing. . . . They traveled to the kouse meadows and the camas prairies . . . and they went into battle together. And finally, they lost the battle together.*

*You see, my friend, the same people who took you from your home took my people from their home. For them, it does not matter that we were here first. More than one hundred years ago, when they wanted us to give up our fathers' land and to move into what they call a "reservation," we fled, with many thousands of brave horses like you to help us.... We went north to find freedom, from Oregon to Idaho, Wyoming, and finally Montana, where we were trapped, so close to freedom. Most of your ancestors were taken from us, or killed, or they ran away, like you did. And my brother thinks that you and your family, up there in the Wilderness, are Nimi'ipuu Sikem—descended from the horses bred by my ancestors and lost during the Flight. So this is why I say that you and I have been friends for a long time.* And the man chuckled softly in the darkness, the bulb of his pipe briefly lighting his face with a warm flare.

*Now the people you ran away from want us to give you back. They have put their mark on you, they say, and now you belong to them. I can tell you it's not a bad life, being with people. My horses are happy, and I treat them well. When they leave me, they go to good homes where they are cared for. But you ... I do not think this life would make you happy, even with me, your friend.*

*I will not give you back to those men, blue filly. And I will not keep you for myself, as much as I'd like to. You must be free. It seems that it is still possible for you, even if it's not for my people.*

As Josiah finished speaking the sad words, he suddenly felt a warm breath in his ear. For a fleeting moment,

Blue nuzzled the man's neck, and his eyes shone over with tears.

. . .

**JOE BOUNCED UP AND DOWN WITH IMPA**-tience, kicking gravel and fidgeting with the truck's door handle. He had never been to the Wilderness before, and that was exciting enough—but more than that, they were going to return the wild mustang to her family! He ran to the barn's entrance yet again, hoping that his grandfather and great-uncle were almost ready to go.

The brothers were finishing a final inspection of the filly. Josiah had worried that she wasn't quite ready for the journey, but Sam and Joe had convinced him, pointing out the mustang's obvious return to health and spirits. Indeed, Blue was in fine fettle—and just as impatient as Joe to get going! A thin network of scars laced her right foreleg and an area of her hindquarters, and a small patch of hair was missing from her forehead where it had collided with the rock in the Snake. She was still a bit sore all over, but that would fade, unlike the scars—and the brand on her neck. Now she had as many markings as her fierce father, and as hard won.

She knew she was leaving this place, and she trusted the man whose hand was on her halter. She trusted that he was taking her home. Her feelings as she practically pranced in place beside him were an unfamiliar brew . . . eagerness to get away, but also sorrow at parting . . . gratitude, but also the feeling of otherness. She was not his kind, and she was not his horses' kind—she was, above all things, wild Blue.

And yet, when the boy approached one last time with a carrot outstretched hopefully, the proud mustang yielded just enough to finally take it from his palm.

· · ·

EZRA PENAHWENONMI RYDER WAS JUST about as excited as Joe, and the number of cups of coffee he'd had while waiting for his friends Sam and Josiah Gray Wolf to arrive only increased his nervous energy.

He heard the sound of wheels pulling into the gas station—probably another customer, but still he went to the door. This time his vigil was rewarded: There was Josiah's shiny red trailer pulling in! Ezra limped—but limped spryly—out the door to greet his friends.

As they shook hands, and Ezra was introduced to Joe, the three men talked over the strange events that had brought them together.

"So you decided not to hand her back to the Bureau," Ezra said, raising an eyebrow to Sam.

"Don't tell me now you disapprove, Ezra," Sam protested.

"'Course I don't. I only called 'em to get the fillies away from those cowboys. The Bureau does a fine service and takes care of a lot of unwanted horses, but like I told you—this herd is special. And I expect that what the Bureau don't know won't hurt 'em." The old man gave Joe a conspiratorial wink, and the boy grinned back at him.

"Well, come see if this really is your wild blue filly," Josiah said, and he led Ezra to the back of the trailer and swung open the top half of the gate.

*Wham!* Despite herself, Blue lashed out a hind leg. She still hated trailers.

"Sure sounds like her." Ezra laughed, peering over the gate. Blue turned her head at the familiar voice and sniffed the air—it was the man who had kept her and Doe the night they were captured! The one who made the funny noises! Blue didn't bother to wonder where he'd come from—maybe there weren't actually that many people in the world. It was a comforting thought, and she relaxed a bit, resigned to waiting in the trailer.

"Sure as shootin', that's her," Ezra said, and he couldn't hide the pleasure in his voice. "Doesn't that just about beat the band? She's come back home. But I bet she's gonna miss her sister. That was a pretty little filly, that was."

"You're as bad as Sam," Josiah commented. "Both sentimental old–"

But seeing the look on his crusty cousin's face, he wisely left the sentence unfinished.

"She'll be all right, Ez," Sam said. "When you told me there were two of them, I called the adoption facility and asked what happened to the red Appaloosa. Pretended like I'd seen her and was interested in buying her. The man told me a family with a little girl had adopted her, real nice folks. Said the red filly took to them pretty quickly. Sweet temperament, he said she had. Not like this wild thing."

. . . .

**AS THE TRAILER BOUNCED ALONG THE OLD** logging road, Blue's heart felt as if it were taking wing in her chest. How long had she dreamed of the smell of home, of the feel of the air of home! Now it was real . . . now it came flooding in through the trailer's high windows: tamarack and mountain stream, honeysuckle and white pine! Some scents were new, but still beloved and familiar–the smell of the Wilderness in late summer, instead of spring, when she had last galloped over these hills. With Doe. And Blue's heart, while lifting high with love—love of freedom, love of family—was also breaking for her sister.

But when the man who was her friend opened the trailer door, all Blue could see was home. She would love it twice as much, for Doe. She paused for a moment to let the man put his cheek against hers. He whispered, *Your sister is in a good place. Go home, my friend.*

And the wild blue filly burst into a canter, then a gallop, the men's voices ringing out behind her, and finally fading away.

*Good luck, darlin'!*

*Don't you let yourself get caught again!*

*Bye, filly! Bye!*

*Go home, my friend!*

And she did.

# EPILOGUE

THE SMALL SPECKLED FOAL WAS GETTING into trouble again.

*Buck! Be careful!* his mother called after him as he careened down the slope, legs scrambling over the last of the winter ice that still lingered in the shady patches of the mountain. Buck pretended not to hear: His uncle and aunt were down by the watering hole, and he wanted to play!

Buck skidded to a halt in front of Shadow and gave her shoulder a joyful head butt. The pale filly curved her neck over her feisty nephew and nibbled his tufty mane affectionately. She looked up to find his mother and whickered a greeting to the blue roan mare now approaching the snowmelt. Like Blue, Shadow still bore a scar from her encounter with men two years ago—a thin hairless groove braceleting her fetlock. But she had grown tall and independent, though joined as closely to her brother Fly as her sisters Blue and Doe had been to each other.

After nuzzling in close to his warm aunt and soaking up a moment more of her gentle attention, Buck charged his uncle Fly, who feigned fright and leaped away, initiating a chase over the hills, sprinkled with early spring wildflowers. As Blue watched them run, she remembered Fly and the band of bachelor stallions playing just like this. But one of them was no longer a bachelor. The blue mare turned to rub her muzzle against the curved crest of the *grullo* who stood beside her, watching their son run free in the warm spring sunshine.

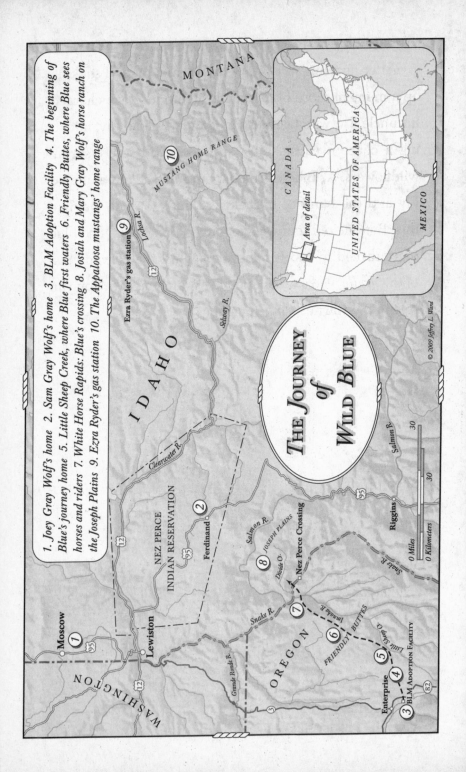

1. Joey Gray Wolf's home  2. Sam Gray Wolf's home  3. BLM Adoption Facility  4. The beginning of Blue's journey home  5. Little Sheep Creek, where Blue first waters  6. Friendly Buttes, where Blue sees horses and riders  7. White Horse Rapids: Blue's crossing  8. Josiah and Mary Gray Wolf's horse ranch on the Joseph Plains  9. Ezra Ryder's gas station  10. The Appaloosa mustangs' home range

THE JOURNEY of WILD BLUE

© 2009 Jeffrey L. Ward

## THE APPALOOSA MUSTANG

A RE THERE STILL WILD HORSES IN THE United States of America? Indeed, there are. They are called "mustangs," from the Spanish word *mesteño,* meaning "wild." In fact, the first modern horses in America came from Spain, sailing over in galleons with explorers in the sixteenth century. Some of the horses the Spaniards brought to help them in their conquests and travels were spotted and splashed with white in dazzling combinations. Eventually, their descendants would be called Appaloosas.

The word "Appaloosa" comes from the area of land in Idaho and Washington near the Palouse River, where Native American tribes, including the Nez Perce, grazed and watered their horses. The Nez Perce, or Nimi'ipuu, a peaceful and prosperous tribe who fished for salmon, hunted buffalo, and harvested camas root, first acquired horses from their southern neighbors, the Shoshones, in the middle of the eighteenth century. By the time the Nez Perce were visited by the explorers Meriwether Lewis and William Clark in 1805, they had become renowned horse breeders, prizing stock that were fleet of foot, had stamina and grit, and especially those mares and stallions that sported the spectacular coats that mark the Appaloosa.

But the peace and prosperity of the Nez Perce were soon threatened by the ever-encroaching Western expansion of the United States. At first, the U.S. government agreed to let the Native American tribe keep seven million acres of their ancestral lands in the area around the conjunction of Idaho, Washington, and Oregon. But then gold was discovered on this Indian "reservation," and white settlers were quick to break the treaty, rushing onto the Nez Perce's land in search for precious metals. In 1863, the government offered the Nez Perce a new treaty that would strip them of all but ten percent of their land. Some Nez Perce, not wanting war, agreed, but others, including the tribes led by Chief Joseph of the Wallowa Valley region, refused to sign. Eventually, war broke out between the U.S. and these "non-treaty" Nez Perce. Chief Joseph led 800 of his people, and about 2,000 of their horses, in a desperate bid for freedom ahead of the advancing U.S. Army. They traveled a grueling, four-month, 1,300-mile march toward Canada, but they were eventually caught and captured in Montana, just south of the border. The survivors of what is known as "the Flight" were forced onto reservations scattered throughout the west, and all of their remaining horses were confiscated by the army.

Could some of the Nez Perce horses have escaped? This was the dream of *Wild Blue: The Story of a Mustang Appaloosa*.

Wild horses still roam parts of the United States, although Ollokot's herd (the stallion was named for Chief Joseph's brother) is fictional. A government agency, the Bureau of Land Management, keeps track of these mustangs, and periodically they round up a portion of the herds and make the horses available for adoption. Until the 1970s, wild horses were often sold for slaughter, but thanks to the efforts of activist Velma Johnson, nicknamed "Wild Horse Annie," Congress passed the Wild Free-Roaming Horse & Burro Act, which says that wild horses and burros may not be captured for slaughter.

There are many books, Web sites, and places to visit to find out more information about mustangs and Appaloosas. Two books that I found most helpful in my research were *America's Last Wild Horses*, by Hope Ryden, and *The American Mustang Guidebook*, by Lisa Dines, which includes information about groups that work to protect our national treasure, including the International Society for the Protection of Mustangs and Burros (www.ispmb.org). The Appaloosa Museum in Moscow, Idaho, has a wealth of fascinating stories, pictures, and artifacts that illuminate the history of the breed (www.appaloosamuseum.org). You can learn more about the Nez Perce at the tribe's Web site (www.nezperce.org), including information about the Young Horseman Project, which is working to reclaim the tribe's age-old prowess with horse breeding and management, including the creation of a new breed of Nez Perce horse, a cross between Appaloosas and Akhal-Tekes, a breed from Central Asia.

The route that Blue travels home from captivity follows roughly the same path as the first part of the Flight of Chief Joseph and his people. There is a Nez Perce National Historic Trail that traces the tribe's full journey, and each year, the Appaloosa Horse Club sponsors a trail ride along a portion of it. The vision of these spotted horses gathered to tread the ground of their ancestors must be something, indeed.

ANNIE WEDEKIND grew up riding horses in Louisville, Kentucky. Since then, she's been in the saddle in every place she's lived, from Rhode Island to New Orleans, South Africa to New York. Her first novel for young readers, *A Horse of Her Own*, was praised by *Kirkus Reviews* as "possibly the most honest horse book since *National Velvet* . . . A champion." She lives with her family in Brooklyn, New York. www.anniewedekind.com